To the Sierra Vista Public Library

The

Maquiladora

Murders

Watch for
The
Monsoon Murders
by
Sydnie Goodell

Treble Heart Books
1284 Overlook Dr.
Sierra Vista, AZ 85635-5512

ISBN: 1-931742-33-2

The Maquiladora Murders

By

Sydnie Goodell

Treble Heart Books

Dedication

To Kathy and Bob and to the memories of Kenny and Jack.

Prologue

The ringing bell roused the security guard from his lethargy. He looked at his wristwatch. It was five a.m.

"Who in the hell," he asked himself, "could be at the loading dock this early in the morning?" He took a quick look at the television monitor. The TV camera scanned the dock area, but the monitor was so hazy he couldn't make out any movement.

He got up from his chair and made his way towards the rear of the building to the Shipping and Receiving Department. He pushed the button raising the dock door, but when he looked outside, the area was empty.

"I'm getting too old for this shit," he muttered. "I just hope I can hold on for two more years."

He was sixty-three years old. His hearing was failing, he needed a cataract operation, and his arthritis was getting worse month after month. The badge on the pocket of his gray uniform shirt read: Joe Wilson, Desert Security.

In two years Joe would retire and then he wouldn't have to worry about security at Dragoon Industries during the hours from midnight until eight in the morning. He normally liked the third shift because there wasn't a whole lot to do except go on his rounds every two hours to make sure no one had gained unauthorized entry and to insure nothing had caught fire. With the advent of flextime at Dragoon, some of the employees came to work around six o'clock when he was just finishing his last round, and they always had time for a little chat. No deliveries arrived until after eight so he didn't have to deal with that. That's when he went off duty.

Joe had just sat down at his desk in the Security Office when the dock bell rang again. He checked his watch and looked at the clock on the lobby wall. It was twenty minutes after five. He stuck his little finger in his right ear and rapidly moved it up and down. Am I hearing things, he wondered, but nevertheless he walked back to the dock again. This time when he raised the door he walked out on the platform and looked around. No one was there. He cocked his head to one side and listened for sounds of some prankster. He heard nothing.

If I tell Desert Security I'm hearing bells, they'll fire me sure as hell, he said to himself, as he walked back to the front of the building. He hadn't even sat down when the bell rang a third time.

"God dammit," he said aloud, and quickly looked around to see if anyone had heard him. Since it was just a little after five, no one else was in the lobby. As fast as his arthritis would allow, he hurried back to the area he had just left. Once again, there was no one on the dock or around the dock door.

"To hell with it," he muttered to himself. "If the damn thing rings again, it'll just have to ring. I gotta go on my rounds."

Chapter One

"W hat d'ya know about Dragoon?" Deputy Beauford Dornan asked his boss as they drove to the administrative offices of Dragoon Industries just outside the town of Sierra Vista in Southeastern Arizona.

"Nothing much," Sheriff Sturling replied, "except they have a maquiladora in Naco, Mexico."

"Oh, yeah. One of them twin plants. Wasn't there an assassination a few years back involvin' one of their people?"

The sheriff nodded. "Yes, the general manager of the maquiladora and his wife were gunned down in a Naco restaurant. The Mexican *federales* were never able to solve the case. I don't think they tried very hard." They drove on in silence for a few minutes and then Sheriff Sturling said, "I take it Dragoon has its own security force?"

"Not exactly their own," Deputy Dornan responded. "They use Desert Security. It's one of them rent-a-cop outfits. Everybody in town calls 'em 'Guards R Us.'"

"When the security guard called he didn't tell you what happened, right?"

"Right. He said something terrible had happened. I tried to press 'im for details, but all he'd say was for you to get out there just as quick as possible."

The deputy left the main road and took a circular drive leading to Dragoon's parking lot. He parked in a visitor's slot, and he and the sheriff got out of the car and stood for a few minutes admiring the three-story building. The architect had designed the adobe brick construction so that a view of the Huachuca Mountains was visible from every office window. The grounds were covered with a pinkish-mauve layer of decomposed granite, and interspersed here and there, along with the native mesquite trees, were various types of cacti and other desert plants requiring only natural rainfall for survival.

The security guard reached for his phone while the two law enforcement officers came through the revolving door.

Lionel B. Sturling, Sheriff of Cochise County for the past twenty years, was a familiar face to most people in Southeastern Arizona. His six-foot, two-inch, 190-pound frame exuded authority and demanded respect. He was approaching his sixtieth birthday, but retirement was something he never thought about. As long as the voters wanted him, he wanted the job.

By the time the sheriff and his deputy had crossed the massive reception area and had been greeted by the security guard, an attractive Black woman walked off the elevator and put out her hand to the sheriff.

"I'm Lisa Webster, Mr. Auchenbach's assistant. Mr. Auchenbach is our Director of Human Resources. Would you come with me, please." The no-nonsense woman turned and addressed the guard, "Let's keep this quiet for the time being."

"Sure thing, Ms. Webster."

"I thought you'd rather not have a bunch of people milling around," Lisa said as the three entered the elevator. "The reason I had the security guard call you is because Mr. Auchenbach is dead."

"Heart attack?" Sturling asked, although he knew he would not have been summoned had that been the case.

Lisa shook her head. "His head is bent forward onto his desk, and I could see blood. I didn't get too close but he didn't look to me like he was breathing. "I think," she hesitated slightly before continuing, "he's been stabbed."

Nothing more was said while the elevator made its way to the third floor. The sheriff and his deputy followed Lisa Webster to a closed door at the end of the hall. A sign above the door read, "HUMAN RESOURCES DEPARTMENT."

"In here," Lisa said, motioning the two men into what appeared to be a waiting room cum secretary's office. A steno desk, complete with the usual word processor and "in and out" trays was situated at a right angle to the doorway. Three four-drawer filing cabinets and several uncomfortable looking chairs were placed against the institutional-beige walls. On each chair was a clipboard with a pencil attached, and under each clip was an application blank with Dragoon Industries' name and logo at the top.

In the room beyond, Sturling and Dornan could see a man sitting in a swivel chair behind a desk. His grey head was resting on the desk blotter. His grey suit coat sleeves covered slack arms hanging at the sides of the chair.

The sheriff looked at Lisa and she nodded her head.

"Yes, that's Mr. Auchenbach."

He walked to the desk and saw rivulets of dried blood clinging to the man's neck, and a dark stain of blood was being absorbed by the blotter. "Not dead too long," he murmured to himself as he searched for a pulse, and at the same time took in the décor of the victim's office.

In sharp contrast to the nondescript outer room with its drab colors and vinyl-tiled floor, Auchenbach's office was covered with plush, deep blue carpeting and the walls were papered in a damask-like covering in soft light blue. "No pulse," the sheriff said as he turned to open the light blue, brocade draperies. The massive mahogany desk was placed to accommodate the best view of the mountains. He glanced at his watch. At this hour in the morning, the Huachuca

Mountains had taken on a pink hue as they basked in the early sunrise. It was only a few minutes after seven. A strange time, the sheriff thought, for the discovery of a recent homicide in a business office.

A credenza, two deep blue, velvet guest chairs, and three potted plants in white wicker jardinières completed the furnishings in Mr. Auchenbach's office.

"Did you touch anything in here this morning, Ms Webster?"

"Nothing but the outside doorknob. I was bringing him a cup of coffee. I knew he was already here. I had seen his car in the parking lot. When I saw him ... like that ... I just backed out of the room. I was pretty shook up, so I called Joe and asked him to get hold of your office."

Sturling couldn't help but think that Lisa Webster looked anything but *shook up*. There was not a hair out place; her make-up had been applied with care; and along with her black and white checkered suit, the crisp white blouse, and black high-heeled shoes, she looked as though she belonged on Wall Street.

"It's just about seven-fifteen," he said as he looked at his watch again. "What time do the employees come to work in the morning?"

"I got here today just a few minutes before seven. I have something personal to attend to after work, and I wanted to get off early." She paused and then continued. "I think I should explain that our work schedule here at Dragoon Industries operates on what is called 'flextime.'"

"I've heard of that," the sheriff said, "but could you explain how it works?"

"Our employees have no fixed hours. Oh, we have established hours within limits, but everyone comes and goes pretty much as they please."

"What sort of limits?"

"Our normal working hours, like most companies, are eight a.m. to five p.m. Flextime allows anyone to come to work between six and nine; put in their eight hours and leave."

"That's interesting," Sturling said, "but how do you know the employees are actually working eight hours? Doesn't anyone cheat?"

"Our security guards keep logs. We all sign in and sign out."

"Then we'll be able to find out what time Mr. Auchenbach arrived this morning."

"Well, I'm afraid not. The executives aren't required to sign the log, only the coolie labor."

"Coolie labor?" The sheriff asked with raised eyebrows.

Lisa smiled, although there was no warmth or humor in the curl on her lips. "Mr. Auchenbach referred to everyone below management level as *coolie labor*."

"I see. Was Mr. Auchenbach in the habit of arriving early?"

"No, he usually came in around nine." Lisa paused again, and then added, "and he usually left around three."

"Do you have any idea why he was here so early this morning?"

"No. It's most unusual. Well, not unusual. It's unheard of."

"Do you think the guard will know when he came in, even though he didn't have to sign the log?"

"Possibly, unless he was making his rounds."

"We'll check with him when we go back downstairs. Beau," the sheriff said, turning to his deputy, "get hold of the medical examiner and an ambulance. You know to keep everyone out of here. Also, leave word at the office for Carlos to get here whenever he returns from Bisbee. Ms. Webster, let's you and I go talk to the guard, and take a look at that log to see who else arrived early this morning."

Chapter Two

1965

Ernesto Garcia waited until nightfall, and then he slept. When he wakened he was hungry, but he could remember having been hungrier. He was certain that when he got to the United States of America he would never be hungry again.

He had been traveling for five days. Sometimes he'd jumped into a boxcar; sometimes he'd begged a ride on a mule-drawn cart; sometimes he'd walked.

At two a.m. the bored border guard started to doze off. Ernesto walked a few feet west of the immigration station, stepped over the downed barbed-wire fence, and slipped into the United States of America.

He saw the lights of a town in the distance, so he went to the northeast, avoiding them. Before long, he came to a small farmhouse. Behind the detached garage was an orchard, the branches of the trees heavily laden with ripe apples. He grabbed one and started eating it. The juice ran out of the corners of his mouth as he devoured the fruit. He licked his lips so as not to miss even a trickle.

Ernesto was so intent on filling his stomach that he almost didn't hear the dog barking. He stuffed more apples into his shirt and pants pockets as he ran. He stumbled once, but was able to crawl over the fence before the dog could reach him. He heard the crack of a rifle, and the dog turned and trotted back towards the farmhouse.

He made his way over to the main road, all the while eating the stolen fruit. Whenever a car came into view, he'd stick out his thumb, but no one stopped. His stomach was starting to ache; those apples hadn't been as ripe as he thought.

He saw an eighteen-wheeler coming down the road and he stuck out his thumb, but the truck drove on past. Then Ernesto heard the air brakes, and the door on the passenger side of the cab swung open. He ran to the truck. The big, brawny man behind the steering wheel held out his hand. Ernesto grabbed it and shook it.

"Get the hell in here," the long-haul driver said. "I'm not tryin' to shake yer hand. I'm tryin' to help you up."

Ernesto didn't understand much English, so he just smiled and said, *"Gracias."*

"Oh, Jesus. Another wetback, huh?"

Ernesto smiled again and said, *"Gracias."*

"I'm goin' as far as St. Louis. Will that help?"

Ernesto nodded. He had heard of St. Louis. He knew it was somewhere in the United States of America.

"Name's Butch Flaherty. Everybody calls me Butch Cassidy. What's year name?"

Ernesto smiled and said, *"Gracias."*

Butch pointed to himself and repeated, "Butch Cassidy."

Ernesto pointed to himself and said, "Ernesto Garcia."

"Ernesto, eh? Well, I think I'll call you Paco."

Ernesto let out a groan and grabbed his stomach.

"You got a bellyache, Paco?" Butch hit the air brakes and his truck rolled to a stop. Ernesto thought his ride had surely been short-lived. "Here," Butch said, reaching into the overhead compartment behind him, "take this." He handed Ernesto a roll of toilet paper. "Go over there behind those trees. I'll wait."

When Ernesto climbed back into the cab, he smiled and said, *"Gracias."*

"Don't mention it. A guy's gotta crap when a guy's gotta crap." Butch turned on the radio and found his favorite country and western station. Over the din of the music, he gave Ernesto the benefit of his views about the problems of the world and politics in general.

"Now the way I figger," he said, "Lyndon Johnson..."

At the mention of LBJ, Ernesto interrupted and said, *"el presidente."*

"That's right, The President. You're a quick study, Paco. As I was sayin', Johnson really goofed up when he didn't drop the bomb on Vietnam."

Ernesto said nothing. He was enjoying the view of the countryside as they rode along together.

"There's a truck stop up the road a ways," Butch said. "I'm gonna pull in and have a hamburger and a cup of coffee. Their food's lousy, but they got a couple of good-lookin' waitresses."

Butch wheeled the truck into the parking lot, got out of his cab, and motioned his passenger to follow him. Ernesto got out, but shook his head. He put his hand on his stomach.

"Your gut still botherin' you, huh? The restroom's over that way," Butch said, and waved his arm toward the east side of the building. He locked the cab and went into the diner. Ernesto headed for the restroom.

Butch took about half an hour for his break, and while he ate he brought his logbook up to date. When he returned to his semi he noticed an apple core lying on the ground by the truck. Paco sure must like apples, he said to himself. He had seen the fruit straining at

Ernesto's pockets. No wonder, Butch mused, he's got a gut ache. I wonder if he eats worms and all?

Butch was glad to have Paco's company as they started rolling again. He could say anything he felt like and not get any backtalk. About midnight his eyes started getting heavy. He pulled off the road into an isolated clearing and grabbed a pillow and blanket from his sleeper. He tossed them to Ernesto and told him he could sleep on the front seat.

"The railroad track runs along on the other side of the road. The train whistle'll wake me up about dawn, and then we'll be on our way." He climbed into the sleeper and drifted off.

Just before first light Butch wakened. He needed to relieve his bladder. He thought about using his relief tube, but abandoned the idea. It was almost time to hit the road again. He started to climb out of the sleeper onto the front seat, but then he remembered his passenger. The cab, however, was empty. Maybe, Butch said to himself, Paco had to take a leak, too.

Butch walked several yards from the truck and had just unzipped his fly when he heard a noise. Two dark figures loomed over him. One struck him on the head, but just before he passed out he saw Paco running from the railroad tracks toward the truck.

When Butch came to, his head was cradled in Ernesto's left arm. Ernesto had gotten the thermos bottle out of the cab, and was trying to get Butch to take a drink.

"Jesus, my head hurts," Butch complained. "What happened to those two guys? Did they take anything out of the van? What's the matter with your hand?"

Ernesto's knuckles were bleeding. "*Vamoose*," was all he said.

Butch gingerly got to his feet and got his first-aid kit out of the cab. He put some Merthiolate on Ernesto's lesions. "Knot's gone down a little," he said as he felt the top of his head. "Good thing they hit me on the hardest part. What in the hell were you doin' over by the railroad tracks?"

"Strawberries," Ernesto answered, and looked down at the ground.

"Who in the world would wanna eat wild strawberries at four o'clock in the morning?" Butch asked. He started to shake his head in wonderment, but remembered how much it still hurt. "Jesus Christ," he exclaimed as he looked at Ernesto. "How could I have been so goddamn stupid? Come on, Paco, we've gotta haul ass. There's a truck stop about fifteen miles from here that makes the best damn breakfast you've ever tasted.

"Well, hi, Butch. Long time no see," the waitress said as she walked up to the booth. "What'll you and your friend have?"

"We both want two eggs over easy, ham, hash browns, sausage gravy and biscuits, and all the coffee you've got in this joint."

"Sounds like you guys haven't eaten for a week."

"Could be," Butch answered, looking thoughtfully at his companion.

Butch turned down the volume on the radio. Ernesto, his appetite finally sated, leaned against the window and was snoring peacefully as they rolled along. He didn't even wake up when Butch stopped at the weigh station just south of St. Louis.

At the truck terminal they unhooked the semi and then drove to the east side of the city. Butch parked his rig in the driveway of a white frame house, and called out as they walked to the front door. "Hey, Marylou, I'm home."

Marylou was Butch's sister. Their parents were both dead, and Butch had paid her college tuition and had made the down payment on the cottage where she lived and where Butch stayed whenever he had to lay over in St. Louis. She was about five foot six and weighed

125 pounds. She was dressed in blue jeans and an oversized blue chambray shirt. Her long black hair was held back from her face with two tortoise shell combs.

"Who's your friend?" she asked, as she reached up and kissed Butch on the cheek.

"Marylou, shake hands with Paco."

She hesitatingly held out her hand and Ernesto grabbed it, pumping her arm up and down.

"Ernesto Garcia," he said, finally letting go of her hand.

Marylou looked quizzically at Butch, and then grinned. "Oh, I get it," she said. "His name is Ernest, but you call him Frank."

Butch returned her grin. "This guy saved the truck, and very likely my life. Is supper ready?"

"It'll be about an hour," Marylou answered. "May I talk to you for a few minutes in private?"

Butch motioned Ernesto to sit down and he followed Marylou into the kitchen.

"Why don't you fill the bathtub and loan him your razor. Butch, he really smells bad. Bring his clothes out, and I'll toss them into the washer and dryer."

"Yeah. Good idea. He is kinda gamey. I had to keep the window down in the cab most of the time since I picked him up."

While Ernesto was bathing and his clothes were being washed and dried, Butch told Marylou how Paco had beaten off the would-be hijackers.

"I think you should see a doctor," Marylou said as she felt the lump on her brother's head.

"Nah," Butch answered. "I'm okay. Just damned lucky I'd picked up Paco."

"Are you certain you shouldn't have your head looked at, Butch?"

"Hey, I know you're a smart schoolmarm. Just stop sounding like one."

Marylou leaned over and gave Butch another kiss on the cheek. "Okay, big brother, you're the boss."

In about an hour Ernesto emerged from the bathroom, clean-shaven and smelling of soap and cologne. His clothes were hardly recognizable. They weren't brown, after all. The detergent had lived up to its advertisements.

"Well, he certainly cleans up nice," Butch said. "I'll help him get a green card, then take him to the warehouse and see if he can get a job in Loading. He's certainly strong enough."

Ernesto paid no attention to Butch and Marylou while they carried on a conversation as though their guest wasn't present. He was busy having two helpings of chicken and dumplings, buttered peas, and cucumber salad.

When they had finished eating and Marylou was clearing the table, she said, "We have pie for dessert." She couldn't understand why Butch and Ernesto both threw their heads back and started laughing uproariously when she added, "its apple."

1970

" I pledge allegiance to the flag of the United States of America," ...Ernesto and fourteen other immigrants recited. He was smiling, but tears were streaming down his face. . . "and to the republic for which it stands. One nation, under God, with liberty and justice for all."

"Congratulations to all of you," the judge announced, "you are now citizens of the United States of America."

Marylou rushed up to Ernesto and kissed away his tears. "I'm so proud of you," she said as she hugged him.

He took her arms from around his neck and held her away from him so he could look at her. "I've put you off long enough. I have an interview tomorrow at Dragoon Industries. If I get the job, we'll get married as soon as I get my first pay check."

* * *

"Ernesto Garcia, eh?" The supervisor of the shipping and receiving department chewed on his cigar as he gave Ernesto the once-over. "You got a green card? I guess you must. Personnel isn't supposed to send any of you guys down here for me to interview unless you've got a green card."

"No, sir. I don't..." Ernesto started.

"Goddammit. Why do they waste my time? Sorry, Buddy, it's not your fault. Under the circumstances I'm afraid we can't use you." The supervisor rose from his chair and started toward the door.

"Mr. Warren," Ernesto said very quietly, reading the supervisor's name from the nameplate on the desk. "I don't need a green card. I'm a citizen. Here's my paper."

1980

"Bud Warren here, Mr. Pizzaro. I know you've been looking for someone to spearhead our maquiladora in Naco, and I think I've got just the man you're looking for."

Ramon Pizzaro, owner of Dragoon Industries, could trace his family tree back to the Conquistadors. He kept it quiet, however, since he wasn't too proud of some of the things that had gone on in Peru during the Inquisition.

His father had started the company sixty years ago. At first, one small plant manufacturing bicycle tire pumps, with five employees comprised Dragoon Industries, but Ramon's father thought BIG. At the beginning of World War II, Dragoon jumped into the war effort, and immediately the company's profits took off. Dragoon was now a ten-billion-dollar a year operation, engaged primarily in manufacturing peripheral equipment for the computer industry. Dragoon's plants were scattered around Europe and in the eastern and southern parts of the U.S., with the headquarters in St. Louis, Missouri.

1990

Ernesto reached over and took Marylou's hand in his. "Happy birthday, sweetheart, and many, many more."

They were having dinner at Los Cantina in Naco, Sonora, the only restaurant of any consequence in this small border town. They had been patronizing the local establishment about once a week since Ernesto had been put in charge of Dragoon's maquiladora.

"Thank you, darling," she said, her eyes shining as she gazed at him. "I just wish you didn't have to go back to St. Louis tomorrow."

"So do I, but I've got to tell Mr. Pizzaro first hand about what's going on down here. At least, what I think is going on."

"But what if you're wrong? I just can't conceive that such horrible things are happening practically in our own backyard."

"I have enough evidence that Mr. Pizzaro—with his clout—can get a formal investigation going."

"Well, at least you'll be back before Arturo gets home for spring break."

"Yes, I can't wait to see him. Who would ever have thought it. The son of an apple thief getting a master's degree."

"Speaking of thieves," Marylou said laughingly, "how much of my cologne did you pour on yourself when you came home with Butch that first time?"

Ernesto looked at her sheepishly. "I'd never smelled anything so delicious in my life. I must have used about half the bottle. I never did replace it, did I? Perhaps this will make up for it." He took a velvet-covered box from his pocket and handed it to Marylou. Her eyes glistened as she bit the corner of her lip.

"Fasten it on me," she said as she stood up. Her eyes were sparkling almost as much as the diamond pendant. Ernesto rose from his chair also and walked behind her to fasten the gold clasp. He didn't notice the crack of the gun until his beloved Marylou slumped to the floor.

A million thoughts raced through his mind: that must have been a shot I heard; what in the world is happening; Marylou is lying on the floor with that ugly hole in her chest; I must buy her some cologne while I'm in St. Louis; that looks like blood oozing from her blouse; Arturo will be home for spring break; why doesn't Marylou get off the floor...

The second bullet shattered Ernesto's brain.

Chapter Three

Joe was standing by the receptionist's desk when L.B. and Lisa got off the elevator. "It's nearing the end of my shift, Ms. Webster," the guard said, "but I thought maybe you'd like for me to stick around for a bit."

"Thanks, Joe, the sheriff needs to ask you some questions."

"Do you know what time Mr. Auchenbach arrived this morning?" L.B. asked the guard.

Joe removed his cap and scratched his head. "No, I didn't see him come in. It musta been while I was makin' my rounds, but the thing is, he never comes in this early."

"What time did you go on your rounds?"

"I started the last one a little before six o'clock. I go up to the third floor on the elevator and work my way down."

"Did you go into Mr. Auchenbach's office?"

"Uh, no. I just looked down the hall toward his office."

"What time was it when you got back to the lobby?"

"Musta been about a quarter to seven." Joe put on his cap and busied himself rearranging the magazines on the receptionist's desk.

"Joe," Lisa broke in, "Sheriff Sturling needs to take a look at this morning's log."

"Let's go in here." Joe picked up the log and pointed to the Security Office. Two walls facing the L-shaped hallway were glassed floor to ceiling, giving the guard on duty full view of the reception area and the elevator. A murky picture scanning the dock and the front door looked back from a television monitor. Lisa reached up and turned a couple of knobs. The picture cleared up. Joe turned the log so L.B. could read it. "A new page is used every time there's a shift change," he explained to the sheriff. "There's twenty-four hour security here: eight to four; four to midnight; and midnight to eight. Everybody signs in and out, except the executives, that is."

"What about visitors, sales people, delivery people?" L.B. asked.

"Visitors and sales reps sign in and out in this book." Joe reached in the bottom desk drawer and handed the sheriff another three-ring binder. "Delivery people have to go 'round back to Shipping and Receiving."

Before L.B. could continue with his questions, a florid faced, stocky man whirled through the revolving doors and descended on the Security Office. "What the hell's going on?" he demanded. "What's the sheriff's car doing in the visitors' lot?"

L.B. and Joe stood up when the man came toward the Security Office. Lisa remained in her chair.

"Mr. Byers," Lisa said, "we have a problem. Mr. Auchenbach is dead. I found him about an hour ago in his office. This is Sheriff Sturling."

Mr. Byers gave L.B.'s hand a perfunctory shake. "So old Charlie died, did he? Too much golf more 'n likely. So why are you here?" he asked L.B.

"It seems," the sheriff replied, "that Mr. Auchenbach was the victim of foul play. And what, may I ask, is your position with Dragoon Industries?"

Mr. Byers's face was getting redder as he looked the sheriff up and down. "I'm the Vice President and General Manager of this division. Everything that goes on around here goes through me. I..."

"Then perhaps," L.B. quietly interrupted, "you can tell us what happened."

"Well, what I mean is," Byers blustered, "I'm responsible for the activities at this division and the profit and loss of the Naco maquiladora. Jesus H. Christ! Now I suppose the home office will be down here messing around. Lisa, I want a full report of what's happened. Get this straightened out as quickly as you can, Sheriff." With that, he turned on his heel and headed for the elevator.

"Uh," Lisa started, "where were we?"

"I was just starting to look at the logs." L.B. had learned long ago not to be impressed with outbursts such as Byers had just displayed, and returned to making some notes from information he found in the logs. "When you get a chance," he asked her, "I'd like a copy of Dragoon's organization chart."

"I'll get it for you right away. Is there anything I can tell Mr. Byers which might soothe him a little?"

"Not at the moment. Excuse me, Ms. Webster," he said as he looked toward the door. "Here comes the medical examiner. I'll need to go back upstairs with him." He headed for the elevator along with the M.E.

"Got a bad one have you, L.B.?" The medical examiner asked, as they rode up to the third floor.

L.B. nodded. "The Director of Human Resources. Stabbed."

The medical examiner gave the body a cursory examination. "Looks like someone did the deed with a small instrument, severing the carotid artery and the jugular vein. May have been dead a couple hours. Rigor's just starting to set in. I'll have a full report in the morning."

While L.B. had been downstairs, Beau had taken Polaroid pictures of the dead man, and had cordoned off the area. Employees, arriving at various times, had heard the news despite Lisa Webster's trying to keep it quiet. They were crowding around Charlie Auchenbach's office trying to get a look at the body. The deputy patiently urged the throng to move along.

Carlos Soto came charging and panting out of the door from the stairwell. L.B.'s Hispanic deputy was five-six and weighed 130 pounds, soaking wet. Beau, on the other hand was six feet tall and weighed right at 200 pounds. When no one was around, Beau called Carlos "Little Buddy." Carlos took the teasing well enough, but no one but Beau could get away with taunting the feisty Mexican-American.

"Hey, Beau, where's the boss?" Carlos asked as he elbowed his way through the throng of spectators.

"In there," Beau said, pointing to Auchenbach's office, "with the coroner. I thought you'd be here before now. Were ya held up in Bisbee?"

"Got here as soon as I could, but some rent-a-cop downstairs made me sign in. Besides, there's a real convention going on around here, and I couldn't get on the elevator. Don't any of these people have offices they're supposed to be in?"

Not waiting for a reply, Carlos held up the yellow tape to walk under it. Several employees tried to follow him. "Can't you read?" he growled. "This is a crime scene. No admittance." He heard one of the employees laughingly say something to the effect that this definitely was a crime scene, but the crowd was dispersing and Carlos couldn't tell who had made the remark.

"Hey," Carlos exclaimed when he walked into Auchenbach's office and looked at the body, "I know this guy."

"What can you tell me about him?" L.B. asked.

"Well, I don't actually *know* him, but he's on the board of directors of the Mexican-American Unity League."

Carlos was a self-ordained ambassador for the Mexican-American community in Sierra Vista. He coached Little League for the young Mexican boys; he helped a local English teacher at night instruct Mexican parents in the English language; and he acted as interpreter for the Mexican-American Unity League, an organization to promote better understanding and co-existence between the Anglos and the Mexicans in Cochise County.

While Carlos was explaining to L.B. his slight association with the deceased, the paramedics arrived. When they attempted to remove the body from the office, another flurry of excitement started in the hallway. Beau cleared the elevator and escorted the paramedics and the stretcher with Auchenbach's body downstairs, out the shipping and receiving dock doors, and into the ambulance. With the removal of the body, the excitement abated. The hallway was practically empty by the time Beau got back to the third floor. Dragoon Industries was resuming business as usual.

Beau and Carlos dusted Auchenbach's office for fingerprints and examined Lisa Webster's office, as well as the secretary's looking for a murder weapon. None was to be found.

L.B. looked through Auchenbach's desk. The middle drawer contained the usual rubber bands, paper clips, pens and pencils, and pads of paper. Another drawer held several golf balls and golf tees. A file drawer in the lower left hand side of the desk contained two folders; one entitled "Personal" and the other, "Damned Personal." The "Personal" file contained one sheet of paper with a list of what the sheriff assumed were golf scores and dates of play. I would have thought, the sheriff said to himself, that his would have been in the "Damned Personal" file. However, that folder contained a sheet of paper with a list of names, with dates or notations appearing after some of the names. The only names he recognized were his deputy's and Lisa Webster's. After Carlos's name were the initials "SAM."

"Carlos, do you know anybody named Sam?" L.B. asked his deputy.

"Not that I recall. I might recognize him if I saw him. Why?"

"Just wondering."

"What's his last name?"

"I don't know. Never mind. I was just curious."

Appearing after Lisa Webster's name were the initials "BAAA." Damned personal or not, L.B. took the sheet of paper from the file folder and stuck it in his pocket.

Lisa Webster ducked under the yellow tape and handed L.B. a piece of paper. "Here's a copy of our organization chart. Is there anything else you need?"

"Just the answers to a few questions, if you don't mind."

Lisa sat down in one of the blue velvet chairs while L.B. was examining the organization chart. "I don't see your name on here, Ms. Webster."

"Only the executives' names and the positions they fill are on the chart. We'd be making a new one every month, otherwise. Our turnover of clerical staff is rather high."

"Why is that? Isn't Dragoon a good place to work?"

"Oh, of course it is. I didn't mean to imply that it isn't, but quite a few of the female clerical staff are married to soldiers at the Fort."

Most people in Sierra Vista and Cochise County referred to Fort Huachuca as "The Fort." The Army outpost had originally been established in the mid-eighteen hundreds to protect settlers from marauding Apaches and to keep the Indians from escaping into Mexico. After many changes throughout the years, the Fort now was the headquarters for the Army Intelligence Center and School and the Army Information Systems Command.

"And, of course," Lisa continued, "their husbands get transferred every few years."

"What about turnover at the maquiladora?"

Lisa frowned. "It's extremely high. I told Mr. Auchenbach we should try to find out why. After all, that's part of Human Resources' responsibilities, but he didn't seem to be too concerned, and in a rather subtle way he told me to mind my own business."

"Mr. Byers mentioned something about the home office. It's in St. Louis, isn't it?"

"Yes, that's where the National Headquarters is located. When Mr. Pizzaro, the owner of the company, decided to start a maquiladora south of the border he also decided the company needed a Southwestern Headquarters, and Sierra Vista is where he chose to build it."

"Why was Mr. Byers so concerned about the home office *messing around*, as I think he put it?"

"Mr. Byers believes that whenever Mr. Pizzaro visits the Southwestern Headquarters, it's a reflection on his—Byers'—management style. That, of course, isn't the case. Byers is just paranoid."

"The people on this organization chart—were they transferred here from St. Louis?"

"Yes. All except Mr. Auchenbach. He was new to the firm. He joined the company about eight months ago."

"Who had his position before he came on board?"

"Sam Babcock."

L.B. started when he heard the name "Sam," and Carlos looked up from his examination of the credenza and frowned.

"What happened to Sam Babcock?"

"Retired. Still lives just outside Sierra Vista. In Yucca Estates, I believe."

"Do you have any idea who might have wanted to kill Mr. Auchenbach?"

"No," she answered and looked directly at the sheriff. Her eyes did not waver, nor did they blink.

"If you don't mind, I'd like for you to go with Deputy Dornan to give Mrs. Auchenbach the tragic news concerning her husband."

"I guess," Lisa sighed, "someone has to do it, and it should be me, I suppose."

* * *

Lisa and Beau left to go convey the news to the widow, and L.B. and Carlos interviewed the employees who, according to the log, had arrived before eight that morning.

Two buyers from the Purchasing Department had come in at six a.m. They explained that flextime gave them the advantage of being able to phone the East Coast early in the day to place orders or negotiate prices. They told L.B. they had gone directly to their respective offices, and had no idea when Mr. Auchenbach had arrived.

Using the Security Office as their interview room, the sheriff and his deputy talked to the other early arrivals and to the first-line supervisors of each department. No one had any idea who would want to do away with Auchenbach. Good old Charlie didn't seem to have any friends within the company, and the answers to L.B.'s questions were vague and evasive.

Carlos was wondering when his boss was going to suggest they break for lunch. It was almost two-thirty. He was just about to say something to the sheriff when four men came through the revolving door. Three of them were dressed in business suits, white shirts, and striped ties. The fourth man was attired in gabardine slacks, a knit sport shirt, and a leather flight jacket.

From the security office, L.B. overheard the guard addressing the casually dressed man. "Mark, have you heard?"

"Yeah. Someone called the airport, and the tower gave us the news before we landed."

L.B. walked out of the security office, and the guard introduced the production manager, sales manager, and purchasing manager.

"We'll be happy to talk to you in our offices, Sheriff," the production manager said. "But I'm afraid there's nothing we can tell you. We've been in St. Louis since day before yesterday."

"I'll probably want to talk to you later. No need right now."

The three managers made their way to the elevator, discussing the death of Mr. Auchenbach in hushed tones.

The security guard introduced L.B. to Mark James, explaining that Mark was the pilot for Dragoon Industries.

"Dragoon has its own plane?" L.B. was impressed.

"Planes," Mark corrected. "We have two small jets."

"I guess with all the traveling, it's easier and more economical to have your own planes."

Mark nodded in agreement. "Saves a lot of time on the ground, too."

"Can you tell me anything about Mr. Auchenbach?" L.B. asked the pilot.

"Couldn't tell you a thing. I hardly knew him. If you'll excuse me, I've got a flight log to fill out."

Chapter Four

"How did Mrs. Auchenbach take the news?" L.B. asked Beau the next morning.

"Well, she was shocked, of course. At first, she didn't want to let Ms. Webster or me come into the house. Just kept lookin' us up and down like we wuz some kind of disease or somethin', but Ms. Webster was cool and sure held her ground," Beau answered, shaking his head and smiling.

"I hope you told her I'd be out to talk to her later."

"Sure thing. She wasn't too pleased when I told her there'd hafta be an autopsy."

"I'd like to see Sam Babcock," L.B. told the guard at the entrance to the condominium complex where the former Director of Human Resources for Dragoon lived.

Yucca Estates had been developed as a retirement community. It consisted of one-story semi-detached homes, a nine-hole golf course, swimming pool, spa, shuffleboard court, and one building used by the residents for arts and crafts. Twenty-four hour security prevented solicitors and other unwanted visitors from disturbing the tenants.

The guard made a phone call, and then instructed the sheriff to proceed on around the circle to the last unit on the right. As L.B. was driving to the Babcock house, he was thinking of an article he had read a few days ago: there are more private policemen in the United States than public law enforcement officers. It seems, he thought to himself, that's certainly becoming true around Cochise County.

"Come in, Sheriff," a white-haired woman said when she answered the door to L.B.'s ring. "I guess you've come because of what happened to Charles Auchenbach."

"Oh, you've heard?" The local paper would not be carrying the story until this evening's edition. L.B. assumed whoever had called the airport was spreading the word.

"Yes, three different people from the office called."

"I'm here to see Sam Babcock. Is your husband in?"

The woman smiled at L.B. "I'm Sam Babcock. I guess," she added when she saw the surprised look on L.B.'s face, "no one told you that Sam is a female. Come on out to the kitchen." She motioned him to follow her and then indicated a chair for him to sit down. She poured them each a cup of coffee. "I was christened *Samantha*," she explained, "but when I was old enough I had my name legally changed. Everyone called me *Sam* anyway, plus I wanted my name to be the same as my father's. But enough about me. What can I do for you?"

"I can't seem to get much information about Charles Auchenbach from the people at Dragoon. I thought maybe you could fill me in."

"You'd better ask questions, then. Otherwise I might go on for hours."

"You had that job before he joined the company. Is that right?"

"Yes, but I had told Mr. Pizzaro and Mr. Byers I was going to retire in a year. They brought Charlie in early so I could acquaint him with the way we did things."

"But you didn't stay out the year?"

Sam laughed. "I'm surprised I stayed two months. It didn't matter how Dragoon did things. Charlie did things Auchenbach's way. The man was...impossible."

"How do you mean?"

"You have to—or should—walk a very thin line when you're in Personnel, or Human Resources as it's now called. If your views lean too much toward management, the rank and file won't trust you. If you try being 'one of the boys' management will think you don't have their interests at heart. Charlie could care less what the people in the trenches thought, as long as he could suck up to management, and he refused to follow written policy. The 'coolie labor'—as he called the clerical and production employees—was always in the wrong, and everyone was out to screw the company, when in fact, he was the one screwing the company."

"You don't seem to have liked him very well."

"It wasn't a matter of *liking* him. The Human Resources Department had lost respect, and I couldn't stay under those conditions. Plus, I was sure there would be some discrimination cases come up which would really put the company in a bad light, and I probably would have been caught right in the middle. Have you talked to anyone who really *liked* him?"

"As I said, I can't get anyone to say anything one way or the other."

"Dragoon is a fine company, Sheriff. Most of the employees are very loyal, and they wouldn't like to say something that would be a black mark against their company."

"How long did you work for Dragoon?"

"Off and on for thirty years. I rose from the ranks, so to speak. My husband was a career army officer, and Dragoon has many divisions—here and abroad—so whenever he was transferred I could usually be transferred also. John, my husband, wanted to retire near Fort Huachuca, and I asked to transfer to Dragoon's Southwestern Headquarters. After John died I decided to retire, too. I didn't intend to leave quite so soon, but..."

"Do you have any idea who would want to kill Auchenbach?"

Sam refilled their cups, and put a plate of warm cinnamon rolls on the table. "Help yourself. I just baked them this morning. I've given a lot of thought to that question since I received those phone calls telling me what happened. Although he wasn't respected, I really can't think of anyone who disliked or hated him enough to kill him."

"Were you at Dragoon when the general manager of the maquiladora and his wife were assassinated in Naco?"

"No, I was at the home office in St. Louis at that time. The case was never solved, was it?"

"The Mexican authorities hauled in a couple of people, but the investigation and the trial were a farce. Do you think there's any connection between what happened to them and Charles Auchenbach's death?"

"He wasn't with Dragoon when that happened, so I don't see how there could be a connection."

"Where did he come from? I mean, where had he worked before?"

"He'd been a consultant, he said. He never talked much about what he'd done, but he let everyone know he'd spent time in Libya, Egypt, and Lebanon."

"Was he hired out of St. Louis?"

"Yes, but he was living here when he came on board. Dragoon checks references very thoroughly, so I have to presume he had impressive credentials. Either that, or he did one hell of a snow job." She smiled and shook her head before continuing. "There was a joke that went around the office for a while: 'I wonder who died in his arms,' meaning Charlie's, of course."

"I guess I don't understand. What does the joke refer to?"

"There's a legend that when old Mr. Pizzaro first started his bicycle pump factory, one of the Pizzaro children became ill and died in the arms of one of the employees. That employee, according to the story, never had to do another lick of work, but he was kept on the payroll. Since Charlie never seemed to do anything of any consequence, someone asked the question: 'I wonder who died in his arms?'"

The doorbell rang and Sam excused herself to answer it. L.B. stood up when another woman entered the kitchen with Sam.

The visitor looked owl-eyed at L.B. before she spoke. "Oh, I didn't realize you had company, Sam. Sorry to bother you."

"Mildred Johnson, meet Sheriff Sturling. We were just having some coffee, but I'm afraid it's all gone," Sam said, standing behind Mildred and pulling a face at L.B.

"How d'ya do," Mildred said as L.B. shook her hand. "I just wondered if I could borrow a cup of flour. I was getting ready to bake some cookies for my granddaughter, and I didn't realize I was out."

Sam poured a cup of flour into a plastic bowl. "Don't bother about returning it. I may need some one of these days myself." She put her hand on Mildred's arm and gently steered her toward the door.

"That's a bunch of nonsense," Sam said when she returned to the kitchen. "She just wanted to find out why you were here. She never bakes cookies for her granddaughter. The child comes over here for cookies whenever she's visiting."

"If they're as delicious as your cinnamon rolls, I can understand why she comes over here." Sam smiled her thanks for the compliment and held out the plate for L.B. to take another roll. "I know I'm taking up a lot of your time," he said as he bit into the warm pastry, "but I'd like to know more about maquiladoras in general. What can you tell me?"

Sam thought about the question for a minute after assuring L.B. that his visit was not an imposition. "Well, you know the word *maquiladora* stands for *twin plant*." L.B. nodded.

"*Maquila* literally means *action*, but originally there was a different connotation. When a miller ground someone else's grain, he would keep a certain amount of the flour as payment for his work. So I guess *maquila* means *performer*—the person who is doing the work. Most of the maquiladora jobs are extremely labor-intensive. That's probably how the name evolved."

"Why did Mr. Pizzaro start a maquiladora in Naco, of all places?"

Sam laughed. "He's never gotten out of his system what his ancestors did to the Inca Empire in Peru while they were looking for El Dorado. The other border towns in Arizona, California, and Texas have been inundated with maquiladoras, but Naco hadn't been discovered, I guess. And as far as having a maquiladora anywhere, remember the labor is cheap. The hourly wage in Dragoon's plants in the United States is about seven times higher than what the workers in Naco earn." They both shook their heads at the inequity.

"I won't bother you any longer, Mrs. Babcock," L.B. said as he stood up. "Thank you for taking the time to talk to me, and for the coffee and rolls. If you think of anything that might help me find out what happened, I'd certainly appreciate your giving me a call." He handed her his card. "I may need to talk to you again later," he added.

"If there's anything I can do to help, let me know. I'm here most days except Thursday. I go to the Desert View Psychiatric Clinic then. I'm a volunteer."

"Carlos, do you know a Sam Babcock?" L.B. asked his deputy.

"No, Boss," Carlos answered. "Why do you keep asking me if I know anybody name *Sam*? I told you before. Never heard of him until that woman at Dragoon mentioned him. Why?"

"Sam's a woman. She used to have the job that Auchenbach had at Dragoon."

"Well, I sure don't know her. What makes you think I do?"

L.B. showed Carlos the list of names he had taken from Auchenbach's "Damned Personal" file. "Your name's on there with *SAM* written after it. Any idea why?"

Carlos scratched his head. "I can't think of any reason why my name's on this list, unless it has something to do with the Mexican-American Unity League. But I don't recognize any of the other names, except for the lady we talked to at Dragoon. Let me make a copy of it and see if I come up with anything."

He made the copy and when he returned to L.B.'s office, he said, "Did you notice that Ms. Webster's name and mine are the only ones which have a notation after them?"

"Yes, I did, but it's probably just a coincidence. Tell me, Carlos, what's the Unity League all about?"

"It's a group of business people from Sierra Vista and around the county, along with some Mexican-Americans who are trying to bring about better relations in the community."

"Sounds like a good idea."

"It is. Among other things, the League tries to help the Mexican population who are unemployed and homeless."

"I hope you're talking about naturalized citizens or those with green cards."

Carlos nodded. "We help them get jobs, tutor them in English, and in general try to keep them from going on welfare."

"What was Auchenbach's role in all this?"

"It never seemed to me like he was really interested in the League. I think the only reason he was on the board of directors was because of his position at Dragoon and the fact that Dragoon has a maquiladora. Good public relations. He missed an awful lot of meetings, and whenever he was present things got a little tense because of his superior attitude."

"How long has the League been in existence?"

"We actually started about three years ago, but it's only really been active for about the last six months."

"Would you like a glass of iced tea, Pound?" L.B. and his wife, Laurie, were sitting on the patio watching the late-September sunset.

Lionel Barrymore Sturling's mother had died during his delivery, and the father, distraught over his wife's death and not paying attention to what he was doing, was killed two days later in an accident at the Lavender Copper Mine. The child was reared, nurtured, loved, and disciplined by his grandmother, Maude Sturling.

Maude was a movie buff, and although she didn't get to see many picture shows, she borrowed such magazines as *Silver Screen* and *Photoplay* from the local library, reading all the gossip about the folks in Hollywood. She was smitten with Lionel Barrymore, and thought her newborn grandson looked exactly like the movie star.

At the time Lionel entered the first grade of Tombstone Elementary School, the kids started calling him "Choo-Choo." He had desperately wanted a Lionel train for Christmas, but Maude couldn't afford it. So after beating up a few of his tormentors, he informed everyone his name was *L.B.*

When he met Laurie in the sixth grade and introduced himself, she promptly told him that "lb" was a pound. The sobriquet stuck, but only she and a few very close friends dared to call the sheriff "Pound Sturling."

"No, I think I'll have a bourbon and water. Join me?"

"Sounds good. Also sounds like you had a hard day."

L.B. didn't comment further, but brought the drinks out to the patio and laid back in a chaise lounge. Neither of them said anything as they sipped their drinks and watched the spectacular array of reds, oranges, and lavenders slowly sinking behind the Huachuca Mountains.

"By the way," Laurie finally said, "what were you doing at Sam Babcock's house today?"

"You know, Laurie," L.B. said, sitting up and shaking his head, "it really amazes me how everyone in this county knows what every other person is doing. How did you find out that I was at Sam Babcock's?"

"Mildred Johnson called to tell me."

"Who's Mildred Johnson?"

"Who's Mildred Johnson?" she mocked. "She said she met you at Sam's today."

"Oh, yes. The woman who came to borrow a cup of flour. What else did she have to say?"

"She just said she'd gone over to Sam's, and that you and she were having coffee and cinnamon rolls. Then she asked me why you were there."

"What did you tell her?"

"I told her you were probably having an affair with Sam."

"Oh, Laurie," L.B. groaned. "Now that'll be all over this end of the county. Did you really say that?"

"Sure. I thought the old dolly needed something spicy to gossip about."

They had gone to bed and L.B. was just beginning to drift off when Laurie nudged him. "You never did answer my question. What were you doing at Sam Babcock's today?"

"I'm having an affair with her," L.B. sleepily mumbled.

"Pound," Laurie said in the darkened bedroom. "One of these days I'm really going to pound you."

Chapter Five

"Mrs. Auchenbach?" L.B. asked the woman who answered the door of the massive, territorial-style house sprawling at the foot of the mountains. He was looking into the brightly protuberant eyes of a hyperthyroid.

"Yes, what is it?" There was no cordiality in Jane Auchenbach's voice. She gave the appearance of just having come from the beauty salon. If anyone touched her head, L.B. thought, her hair would crack. Most of the housewives the sheriff was acquainted with wore shorts or jeans, even when they did their grocery shopping, but the woman he faced was attired in a silk dress, hose, and high-heeled shoes. Her jewelry consisted of a single strand of pearls, with matching earrings. Perhaps, he thought, she was on her way to a committee meeting or to do lunch with one of her equally bored friends. She certainly didn't look as though she was mourning the death of her husband.

"I'm Sheriff Sturling. I think you've already met my deputy, Beauford Dornan."

"Yes," she snarled, as she looked at Beau, "when he was here with that...woman."

"Afternoon, Ma'am," Beau tipped his hat as he spoke, but Jane Auchenbach ignored him. Her eyes were focused on L.B.

"What is it?" she repeated.

"We need to ask you some questions about your husband, and also we need to examine his study, or den, or whatever to see if there's anything which can throw some light on his..."

"Do you have a search warrant?"

L.B. took the official document from his pocket and handed it to her. She spent several minutes making a pretense of reading all the fine print, and without saying a word, motioned L.B. and Beau into the house.

"The library is down here." They followed her down a hall and entered a room which L.B. would hardly call a library. One five-shelf bookcase about three-feet wide was filled with dog-eared paperbacks, and after a quick look at a couple of titles, he discerned that Charlie's literary taste certainly wasn't bent to the classics. A large oak desk faced a bay window which looked out at the mountains. A reclining swivel chair, two wing chairs, and a four-drawer filing cabinet comprised the balance of the furnishings.

Mrs. Auchenbach rigidly sat down in the swivel recliner, and turned to face the two law enforcement officers. "What is it you wish to know?"

Without waiting for an invitation, L.B. and Beau each sat down in one of the wing chairs. Beau took a notebook and pencil from his pocket.

"When was the last time you saw your husband?" L.B. asked.

"Yesterday," she snapped. "At the mortuary."

"Look, Mrs. Auchenbach," L.B. said, suppressing a sigh, "you can be as hostile as you wish, but we *are* investigating a murder. If you cooperate, perhaps we can get this thing cleared up soon. Or, if you prefer, we can go to my office and drag it out for a long time, but we *will* get our answers. Now, when is the last time you saw your husband *alive*?"

She glared at L.B. and then at Beau. "Tuesday. In the evening. He went to bed shortly after dinner. We dine about eight."

"Do you know why he went to the office so early Wednesday morning? I understand he usually didn't arrive there until around nine."

"He probably had an appointment."

"Did he mention an appointment? Did he say who with?"

Mrs. Auchenbach shook her head. "Charlie was involved in so many things. He was on the board of several companies, you know. So the appointment could have been with anybody."

"Did he have any enemies that you know of?"

"Oh, no. Everyone thought the world of Charlie."

Not quite everyone, L.B. thought. He had gotten up from his chair and had walked over to the desk. "I notice there are two telephones here on the desk. May I ask why?"

"That one," she pointed to a beige push-button instrument, "is an extension to the one in the kitchen and the bedrooms. The other one is...was...Charlie's private phone."

Charlie's private phone consisted of two lines, with a "hold" button, "call waiting," and "redial." L.B. nodded to Beau, who copied down the numbers appearing over the separate lines.

"I just remembered," Mrs. Auchenbach said, "Charlie had said he wanted to have his private phone removed. I guess I can go ahead and have that done now."

"I'd rather you didn't have it removed for the time being," L.B. said. "I think you'd better leave everything just as it is for now. If I may disturb you, we'd like to go through his desk and filing cabinet."

She moved to one of the wing chairs, but never took her eyes off L.B. and Beau as they methodically went about their search.

The desk was as devoid of information as was Charlie's desk at Dragoon Industries. File folders in the filing cabinet were entitled with names of all those things Charlie had been involved with: Barber Amalgamated, Albuquerque, New Mexico, where he was on the board of directors; Sierra Vista Chamber of Commerce, where he represented Dragoon; Mexican-American Unity League, member of the board; Thunder Mountain Hospital, Sierra Vista, member of the board; United Way, Sierra Vista, again representing Dragoon. Nothing held a clue as to Charlie's untimely demise.

A file folder bearing the name "Maquila" was out of alphabetical order. It had been placed at the back of the drawer. It contained several sheets of paper, listing what appeared to be names of Hispanics. Some of the names were crossed out, some had question marks after them, and after each name was what appeared to be a date. L.B. assumed it was a list of potential employees for Dragoon's maquiladora. But why, he wondered, did Auchenbach have the list here at his home rather than in his office? From what he had learned of Charlie, he didn't seem the type to take his work home.

"I'm going to take this folder with me," he told Mrs. Auchenbach. "Beau will write out a receipt for you."

When Beau offered the receipt to Jane, she snatched it from his hand. "Is that all?" she demanded.

"I think so for the time being," L.B. answered. "We may need to talk to you later, however."

"I plan to have the cremation as soon as you release the body, and then I'm going to New York to visit my sister."

"I think you'd better not leave town, for the time being, at least."

"Then maybe I'll ask my sister to come here." For the first time she showed a modicum of emotion. "I feel so alone with Charlie gone."

L.B. wondered just how lonely she was with Charlie gone. She'd given the impression that good old Charlie wasn't around much of the time.

On L.B.'s instructions, Carlos interviewed the employees at Dragoon's maquiladora in Naco, Sonora, Mexico. The plant manager had given the deputy permission to talk to the hourly employees while they were working. Since the boss didn't understand much Spanish, he didn't stay around the production area, but the lead man, Hernando Rodriquez, was conversant in both languages and hovered nearby.

None of the workers knew anything about Charlie Auchenbach, other than they were aware he was a big shot. He didn't come into the twin plant all that often. They all liked working for Dragoon, they said, but none of them had been employed very long. Many of them had come from southern Mexico, hearing about employment opportunities from their friends or relatives.

Carlos's curiosity was piqued. He couldn't understand why some of the employees had come to Naco from as far away as Oaxaca, some 2500 miles from Naco.

"How did you happen to come way up here?" Carlos asked a young man from Oaxaca who was placing tiny components onto a printed circuit board. "Wouldn't one of the other maquiladoras been closer to home?"

"My cousin used to work here," the young Mexican said. "He told me he would be leaving soon to go to the United States, and that I could take his place. Some day soon," he said, as he smiled at Carlos, "I am going to the United States, also."

Carlos was third generation Mexican-American, and as such was not pleased with the illegal immigration which was running rampant in Texas, New Mexico, and California, as well as Arizona. "Have you heard from your cousin lately?" he asked the young man.

"No, I haven't heard from him since he left. Juanita's sister," he nodded to the young woman sitting across from him, "left at the same time, and I think maybe they might have gotten married." He laughed as he added, "They're probably too busy to write or call."

Juanita looked up at Carlos as though to say something, but Hernando walked up behind her, and she hurriedly bent over her task.

Carlos waited a few minutes until Hernando was called away before asking another question. "Does your cousin have other family in the U.S.? Someone who is going to sponsor him?"

"According to what he told me, there are some people who help Mexicans get their U.S. citizenship. Then he'll be able to get a better job, making more money than he made here. He'll be able to send some back to his family."

During his questioning, whenever Hernando was out of earshot, Carlos learned that most of the employees had taken the place of friends or family who had immigrated to the United States.

"It seems to me," Carlos said to Hernando when the lead man returned to the area, "that the employee turnover here is really high."

Hernando made no response to Carlos's comment, and merely shrugged his shoulders.

"Doesn't it bother you to have to train these workers only to have them leave in a few months?"

"There are always more where they came from," Hernando answered. And besides," he added, "what's our turnover got to do with Auchenbach's murder?"

"Nothing, I guess. I was just curious."

Carlos parked his car at the end of the street, and waited in it until the maquiladora's shift ended. The workers were all hurrying home, and he watched the lead man get in a pickup and drive away. Soon afterwards, Juanita came out of the building and looked up and down the street. She spotted Carlos, and ran to his car.

"May I speak to you?" she asked him in Spanish.

"I thought maybe you had something to tell me. I've been waiting for you." He reached across the front seat and opened the passenger door. Juanita ran around the car and scooted into it.

"It's about my sister." She started talking before she had closed the door.

"The one who went to the United States with that fellow's cousin?"

Juanita nodded. "Yes. Gabriella. You see, when she left she told me she would call me at the *candida* to tell me how things were going.

I am to wait there every night for her call." By now, the street was deserted, but Juanita kept searching it as her eyes raced up and down the street.

"Go on," Carlos urged.

"When she becomes a citizen she is going to send for me. The thing is, she hasn't called. I'm afraid she may not have passed her physical exam."

Carlos was almost certain that the maquiladora workers who had gone to the U.S. were not immigrating under legal procedures. He was sure they were sneaking in and becoming part of that vast group of illegal immigrants, who if caught by the border patrol, were immediately returned to Mexico. Still, he thought, if Juanita's sister is concerned about passing a physical exam...

"You know," Juanita continued, "the physical she has to take before she can even start studying to become a United States citizen."

Before she can even start studying? Surely, Carlos thought, Juanita or Gabriella must have misunderstood. "What makes you think she might not pass the physical exam?"

"When Gabriella was very young she contracted hepatitis. Oh, not from drugs or needles," she hurriedly added. "It was caused by the water where we lived." Juanita hung her head, remembering the sordid circumstances of her childhood. "She has to watch her diet, get plenty of rest, and she can drink no alcohol. It's her liver which flares up if she isn't careful." Juanita furtively watched the street as she spoke. "She might not have been able to fool the doctor who examined her. But if she didn't pass the physical, and has to come back to Mexico, why hasn't she gotten in touch with me?"

"Juanita," Carlos asked, making no attempt to answer her question, "are you looking for someone? Are you frightened that somebody will see you talking to me?"

"Yes. Hernando."

"I saw him drive away just before you came out of the plant. Why would he mind if we talk to each other?"

"He was very angry when you left. He told all of us not to talk to you again if we valued our jobs. He said we would be blamed for what happened to Mr. Auchenbach."

Chapter Six

L.B. checked the names in Dragoon's Visitors' Log, and after a few phone calls determined that none of the people listed had anything to do with the Human Resources Department.

He, Carlos, and Beau interviewed all the top echelon at Dragoon Industries. When they asked if Auchenbach had any known enemies, no one knew of any, but it was suggested they could save time if they looked for any friends Charlie might have had. Dragoon Industries was certainly not mourning its late Director of Human Resources.

Once again the sheriff singled out Lisa Webster. "How did you get along with Mr. Auchenbach?" he asked, emphasizing *you*.

"We tolerated each other," was her curt reply.

"He must have thought a lot of your abilities to promote you into the position you now have." This tidbit of information had been picked up from one of the other interviews.

"Oh, come on, Sheriff. Be realistic."

"What do you mean?"

"I was put in the position to make the Southwestern Division of Dragoon look good for its affirmative action program."

"Do you mean you're not really qualified to handle the job?"

"I think I'm qualified, and I work damn hard, but I also know Charlie had an ulterior motive."

"Like what?"

"Well, let's face it. First of all, I'm black. That's pretty obvious. Also, I'm female."

"That's obvious also."

She shot a quick look at L.B., and then smiled. "I'll take that as a compliment."

"You should. But what was this *ulterior motive*?"

"Auchenbach put me in this position to make a point. You see, my husband is stationed at Fort Huachuca. Nothing's certain in the Army, and we never know when Glen may be transferred." Lisa stifled a sigh before she continued. "Charlie, knowing the situation with my husband, promotes me into a quasi-managerial position. If, in six months or so I have to resign to go with my husband when he's reassigned, Auchenbach will be able to make his point."

L.B. was still puzzled by her explanation. "What point was Charles Auchenbach trying to make?"

"At first, Charlie balked at hiring and promoting minorities, but Mr. Byers, who can be pretty persuasive, pressured him. So, the point being, Charlie could say, 'I told you so.' I can just hear him telling Mr. Byers that you can't depend on minorities, especially female minorities."

"Was Charlie a bigot?"

"One of the biggest bigots who was ever begot, if you'll pardon the alliteration."

L.B. had the feeling Lisa wanted to keep talking. "What else can you tell me about him?" he asked.

"In addition to being a bigot, he was also a lech. Oh, I don't mean he ever made a pass at me," she interjected when she saw the look on L.B.'s face. "We had three different secretaries in this office the first six weeks he was here. The first two didn't give notice—just walked out, but I caught up with the last one when she, too, was leaving unannounced. When I asked her what had happened she started crying. I took her into the cafeteria, and after she quit crying and settled down, she told me some things I'd rather not go into. They were disgusting!"

"And there was nothing you could do about it."

"If I didn't think so much of Dragoon Industries, I would have encouraged her to file a sexual harassment suit, but I couldn't do that. Part of my job is to keep things like that from happening."

"Was the sexual harassment still going on at the time he was murdered?" L.B. remembered Sam Babcock's remark that she felt sure there would be some discrimination suits filed.

"Not to my knowledge. Charlie had tried to get girls who were white and good-looking from other departments to transfer to Human Resources. Mr. Byers got wind of it and I heard him tell Charlie in no uncertain terms to stop pirating labor. He also told Charlie to get an elderly and homely secretary for his department."

"I haven't seen anyone at the secretary's desk in your office. Did he hire an elderly and homely secretary?"

"Mrs. Adams, our secretary, isn't homely, but she's in her late fifties. She's been on personal leave for the past week."

"I'll need the names and addresses of the three women who walked out."

"I know what you're thinking, Sheriff, but they no longer live in Sierra Vista. One of them got married and moved to Phoenix, and the other two have gone to California. I've already checked."

L.B. sighed. "That takes care of that, I guess. Will you be promoted into the position Auchenbach held?"

"No, Sheriff. I've already told Mr. Byers that Glen and I are going to have a baby. We've known for three months, but I hadn't announced it until today. I have no intention of returning to work. So you see, I had no reason to do away with good old Charlie."

As L.B. got off the elevator and entered the lobby, a stately, gray-haired gentleman walked through the revolving door, followed by Mark James, the pilot. James nodded to L.B., and headed for the elevator.

The gentleman put out his hand to L.B. "I'm Ramon Pizzaro. I take it you're L.B. Sturling, the sheriff."

"That's correct. I'm glad to meet you, Mr. Pizzaro. I've been wanting to talk to you."

"Let's go into the conference room over here where we won't be disturbed."

Mr. Pizzaro led the way, and they entered a large room off the lobby furnished with three long sofas covered in brushstroke prints facing each other, forming a U. Southwestern lamps sat on stone tables, and Navajo rugs were scattered over the stone-tiled floor.

"So," Pizzaro said as the two men were sitting down, "lightening does strike twice in the same place, doesn't it?"

"Not exactly in the same place. I take it you're referring to the assassination in Naco of your plant manager and his wife."

"Yes," Pizzaro nodded, "I am. Granted, not the same place exactly, but nevertheless, the same company. Close enough, I'd say. What do you make of all this?"

"Do you think there's a connection with Mr. Auchenbach's murder and what happened five years ago?"

"I really don't know what to think." Pizzaro shook his head as he talked. "That killing in Naco was so bizarre." Ramon Pizzaro went on the explain to L.B. how Ernesto Garcia had come to the United States, learned English, gotten his citizenship, married Marylou, and how he had risen in the company and had become general manager of the Naco maquiladora.

"The strange thing, Sheriff,—and I told this to the Mexican authorities at the time—Ernesto had telephoned me earlier the day he and his wife were shot. He said he had to talk to me in person about something terrible he felt certain was going on, but he didn't want to discuss it over the phone."

"Did he give you any inkling as to what it was?"

Pizzaro shook his head. "He said he was afraid Dragoon might become involved if there was an investigation. But in his words, 'What I think is going on is so horrible, you won't believe it.' We arranged for him to fly to St. Louis the next day, but he never got to make the flight."

"And you never found out what was bothering him?"

"I made all sorts of inquiries. The Mexican *federales* just seemed to chalk up the shootings to another random killing. No one here at the Southwestern Headquarters or at the maquiladora had any idea what he was concerned about. For a while I thought he had been mistaken. Dragoon was never under any sort of an investigation. But then, why were he and his wife murdered? I never bought the 'random killing' theory."

"As I remember it, I thought her murder was an accident. I was told the assassins were aiming at him, but she stood up just in time to catch the bullet."

"I think that's what it was meant to look like. Anyone who knew Ernesto and Marylou, and their devotion to each other, would have known they never kept anything from each other."

"There is a son, isn't there?"

"Yes. Arturo is just finishing his master's degree now. I asked him at the time if he knew what was bothering his father, but he was in the dark. I'm afraid we'll never find out."

"Tell me about Auchenbach," L.B. asked. "I can't seem to get anyone to give me any information about him."

"As a matter of fact," Pizzaro said, "I was planning on letting him go shortly. Now I'll have to get his replacement sooner than I anticipated."

"Why were you going to fire him, if I may ask?"

"He rubbed people the wrong way, and was anything but empathetic with the rank and file. Charles Auchenbach certainly was not one whom you would call *politically correct*."

"You didn't realize his shortcomings when you hired him?"

Pizzaro shook his head. "Sam Babcock—have you met her?" L.B. nodded. "Fine woman," Pizzaro continued. "Sam was getting ready to retire, and I wanted someone on board before she left. Auchenbach's resume looked good. He'd spent a lot of time with firms in Lebanon, Egypt, and Libya as a consultant. I spoke on the phone to his local references, and they gave glowing accounts."

"Oh, he'd worked in Sierra Vista before joining Dragoon?"

"Yes, again as a consultant for two small companies. I can't remember their names right off hand, but if that's important, I can get them for you."

"I'd appreciate that."

L.B. asked the guard where he might find the company pilot. He was told Mark James was probably in the cafeteria having a cup of coffee.

The sheriff walked down the hall toward a door marked *Cafeteria* and saw the pilot sitting at a table, looking first out toward the Huachucas and then at something he had in his hand. Sliding glass doors provided an excellent view of the mountains, but Mark looked as though he were a thousand miles beyond them.

L.B. got himself a cup of coffee, paid the cashier, and walked over to where Mark was sitting. "May I join you?" he asked.

Mark was startled out of his reverie, but nodded. L.B. sat down. The pilot tried to put what he was holding in his hand into his shirt pocket, but a photograph slipped out of his hand and landed face-up onto the table. L.B. saw the picture of a stunning redheaded woman with green eyes and a dimple in her chin. "Your wife?" he asked the pilot.

Mark nodded, picked up the photo, and put it in his wallet.

"Gorgeous day, isn't it?" L.B. asked, and again Mark nodded. The sheriff realized the pilot wasn't in the mood for small talk, but

L.B. went on anyway. "Tell me," he persisted, "Did Mr. Auchenbach utilize the company plane often?"

"Not too often, unless several executives were going to the same destination."

"Do the executives always fly in the company plane when they're on company business?"

"Not always. If only one guy is going somewhere and there's a commercial connection, it isn't economical to use the company plane."

"No, I guess it wouldn't be. So you never got to know Charles Auchenbach too well, did you?"

"No. Sorry I can't help you." With that, Mark walked out of the cafeteria leaving L.B. with a cup of cold coffee.

"Arturo Garcia, you're wanted on the phone," a graduate student yelled down the hall of the dormitory.

"This is Arturo Garcia," the son of Ernesto and Marylou said as he picked up the receiver from the hall phone.

"Ramon Pizzaro here."

"Yes, Sir. What can I do for you?" Arturo asked.

"When will you complete your finals?"

"They're completed. I've just finished packing."

"We have a management opening at our Southwestern Headquarters. Are you interested?"

"Of course. I'll be on the next plane."

"You can't make very good connections from there. Just stay put for tonight. The company plane will pick you up tomorrow morning about ten o'clock."

Chapter Seven

"Y our wife's on the phone, Sheriff."

L.B.'s secretary had not gotten the words out of her mouth before he grabbed the phone. In the twenty years he had been Sheriff of Cochise County, Laurie had only called him at work two times: once, when her mother had died, and again when she was having an attack of appendicitis and had finally phoned L.B. to take her to the hospital.

"Are you all right? Is something wrong?"

"Oh, Pound honey, I'm sorry to bother you at work.

"What is it?"

"Mildred Johnson just called me again."

"Oh, no," L.B. groaned. "Now look, I promise I haven't been visiting any more ladies at Yucca Estates."

"I know. She called because she's concerned about Sam Babcock."

"Why?"

"It seems Sam jogs around the condominium complex every day, but Mildred hasn't seen her for two or three days."

"What's so unusual about that? Maybe Sam went away for a while."

"Mildred doesn't think so. The residents at Yucca Estates are supposed to tell the security people if they're going to be gone for a few days or overnight. That way the guards can keep an eye on things for them. Sam didn't notify the guards that she was going away. They haven't seen anything of her either. They've phoned the house and Mildred has been trying to call Sam, but there's no answer."

"Do the guards have keys to the units?"

"Yes, but they aren't supposed to go into any of the houses unless some member of the family thinks something's wrong, or if someone smells smoke, for instance. Mildred's really worried. She thinks Sam may have had an accident or that she's sick. She thought you could probably get the guard to unlock the door since you're the sheriff."

"I don't know. It seems rather presumptuous to me."

"You could just drop by and talk to the guard. I know Mildred's a gossip and she may be making something out of nothing, but still..."

"Okay. I'll knock off early and stop there on my way home."

"Please call Mrs. Babcock and ask her if she has time to see me," L.B. said to the guard when he stopped at the entrance to Yucca Estates.

"I'll call, but she hasn't been answering the phone all day." The guard made the call, but shook his head and hung up the phone after a few minutes.

"I understand you haven't seen her for a few days."

The guard nodded. "That's right. I asked the guys on the other shifts, and they haven't seen her either. She jogs a lot, but no one has seen her for the last couple of days."

"Could she have gone on a trip and not let you know?"

"I don't think she'd do that without letting us know. She's always told us before. Everybody does. That way we can keep an extra eye out on their unit."

"Does she have any relatives around close?"

"Not that I know of." The guard opened a notebook on his desk, scanned a couple of pages and looked up at L.B. "under the section 'In Case of Emergency Notify,' it says 'only in the event of death,' and there's the name of a nephew who lives in England. Here," he said, turning the notebook around so L.B. could read it.

L.B. made a note of the name and address and then said, "I think it might be a good idea if you and I unlocked her door to see if everything's okay."

"Gee, Sheriff, I'm glad you said that. I've been concerned ever since Mrs. Johnson mentioned Mrs. Babcock's absence. But I can't instigate an entry on my own unless I smell smoke or something."

"All right, then. Let's do it."

"Can you hold on for about five minutes? The next shift starts at four. Oh, here he comes now."

The guard hurriedly explained to the relief man what was going on, and got into L.B.'s car. They drove around the circle and parked in front of Sam Babcock's unit.

"Unlock the door," L.B. told the guard, "and then keep that woman out of here." He had seen Mildred Johnson hurrying across the street to be in on any excitement.

As he walked into the house he called out, but there was no answer. In the living room, dining alcove, and kitchen, everything looked the same as it had on his first visit. There were no dirty dishes in the sink, and no accumulated dust. He walked down a hall to what was probably a bedroom. The bed was made; there were no drawers pulled out. The door to another room was closed. He thought it was probably a den or a study. He took a handkerchief from his pocket and turned the doorknob.

Sam Babcock was slumped over her desk much the same as Charlie Auchenbach had been found in his office. The air conditioning in the condo helped to control the stench emanating from the decomposing body. Dried blood had run onto the desk from Sam's neck, apparently out of the carotid artery.

* * *

The medical examiner and paramedics arrived shortly after L.B. called them.

"Looks like the same sort of instrument as the one used on the fellow at Dragoon," the M.E. said. "Who is she, L.B.?"

"Her name's Sam Babcock. She's the former Director of Human Resources at Dragoon. Charles Auchenbach took her place when she retired."

"If it weren't so bizarre," the M.E. said, "it'd look like it was open season on Human Resource Directors. What in the hell do you think is going on?"

"I wish I knew." L.B. got his camera out of the car, ignoring Mildred Johnson's questions, and took Polaroid shots of Sam and the room in general. "Go ahead and get the body out of here," he told the M.E., "and let me know if you can figure out how long she's been dead."

Carlos and Beau arrived just as the paramedics were loading Sam's body into the ambulance.

"Who was she? Carlos asked.

"Sam Babcock," L.B. answered and looked at Carlos for some sign of recognition.

"No, Boss, before you ask again, I don't know her."

Beau and Carlos set about doing their usual thing: they cordoned off the house, dusted the area for fingerprints, and went through everything looking for clues.

"There are no loose window screens and the doors certainly don't look like they were forced," Carlos said when he came back inside after examining the outside of the house.

"Check with the guards," L.B. told Carlos. "Find out if the other residents can vouch for any visitors they've had in the last few days. Also find out what kind of service people have come into the complex the last couple or three days."

L.B. walked back to the study where he had found Sam's body. Beau had gone through her desk, but found nothing to throw any light on the murder. "Did you take a look at her calendar?" L.B. asked, pointing to the opened book by the telephone.

"Yeah, but she musta doodled a lot while she was on the phone. There's a lot of chicken scratches alongside her appointments. The letters *DV* appear on each Thursday page."

"She told me she was a volunteer at the Desert View Mental Health Clinic every Thursday. Anything else?"

"No, just hair appointments and dental appointments. Nothing to get excited about."

"I guess I should be happy Mildred Johnson is such a snoop," L.B. said to Laurie after he had told her about finding Sam Babcock's body.

"That poor woman," Laurie murmured. "I mean Sam, not Mildred. There is a connection to the Dragoon murders, isn't there, Pound?"

"I would think Sam had been retired too long for the two murders to have a corporate connection. I wish I'd talked to her in more depth before this tragedy happened."

"You mentioned the only relative lives in England, right?"

"Yes, a nephew. I'll have to get in touch with him. I guess my only hope is to talk to the people at the mental health clinic where she was a volunteer. Maybe they can tell me something about her."

The administrator at Desert View Mental Health Clinic was reluctant to give out information on a volunteer. You'd think, L.B. thought to himself, that I was asking about a patient.

Finally, he managed to find out that Sam volunteered her time every Thursday from nine a.m. to four p.m. She had no contact with the patients. She sorted mail for the several on-call psychiatrists and psychologists; answered the phones and made appointments; completed various insurance forms; and, it seemed to L.B., did all the office work the paid help didn't want to do.

She had been a volunteer for a little over six months. Everyone she worked with at the clinic seemed to like her, but had no social contact with her. No one had any idea who would want to do bodily harm to Sam Babcock.

According to the M.E., Sam had been dead about two days. No service people—landscapers, pest control route men, telephone technicians, or what-have-you—had made a service call to Yucca Estates during that time.

Three residents had had personal visitors, but they had stayed only a couple of hours and had not left the units they were visiting until they departed the complex.

Chapter Eight

Beau was just hanging up the phone as the sheriff walked into his office. "We just had a call," he said to L.B. "A woman's body has been found in the ditch out on Highway 92, south of Nicksville. Sounds like a hit and run."

"That's all we need on top of everything else," L.B. said. "You and Carlos get out there right away. I'll call the M.E. and ambulance, and have them meet you there."

"I'm the one who called the sheriff's office," an excited man told the two deputies as he waved them down. He'd gotten out of a late-model white Lexus. Beau and Carlos could see perspiration stains on his shirt. He was wiping sweat from his forehead. "I have a cellular phone, and when I saw what it was, I called. Name's Donald Norman. I live in Bisbee. Have a law practice there, but was on my way to Sierra Vista. I haven't touched her...or anything else." Donald Norman finally wound down, and leaned against the side of his automobile as though he were exhausted.

Carlos walked over to the ditch where a woman was lying prone, with her head at a right angle to her body. Her neck was broken. She was wearing a multi-colored cotton skirt and a white blouse. Her arms and legs were splayed like a bird in flight. She had on canvas sneakers, but no stockings. Her only jewelry was a tiny cross on a silver chain around her neck. No handbag was in sight.

"How did you happen to see her?" Beau asked. He noticed Norman's eyes darting back and forth between the dead woman and Carlos.

"I really don't know. Something—it must have been the white blouse or, oh hell, I just don't know—something caught the corner of my eye. I stopped and backed up a few feet. I got out of the car and saw her. I really don't want to get involved. If it's okay with you, I'll just be on my way." He started to get into his Lexus.

"Hold on just a minute," Beau said. "Where did you say you were goin' in Sierra Vista?"

"I have an appointment with Spencer Motors to have my car serviced."

Beau called Spencer Motors and they verified that, indeed, Donald Norman had an appointment for service on his Lexus, but he was late. Then Beau called the Department of Motor Vehicles and verified the license number and registration of the car Norman was driving. After writing down Norman's home and business addresses and phone numbers, he told the man to be on his way.

The ambulance and the medical examiner arrived at almost the same time. Donald Norman got the hell out of the area, and Beau directed what little traffic there was, urging the few curious passing motorists to keep on driving.

When the M.E. turned the body over he called Carlos to take a look. "She's Mexican. Do you know her?"

Carlos gave the medical examiner a scathing look. "It may come as a surprise to you, but I don't know every Mexican in Cochise County."

"Oh, come off it, Deputy Soto," the coroner countered. "Don't be so damned touchy. Do you know her?"

Carlos had not been hired by L.B. to fulfill an affirmative action goal. He had been the most qualified person the sheriff had interviewed, and he was invaluable in helping with the language barrier when the sheriff's department had to deal with the many Mexicans migrating into or passing through Sierra Vista.

Deputy Soto could trace his family back to the days of Pancho Villa. His great-grandfather had ridden with Villa when the infamous raid was made on Columbus, New Mexico. His great-grandfather was wounded, left behind, and nursed back to health by a good Samaritan in in Columbus. The Soto family had been in the U.S. ever since.

Carlos was a proud Mexican-American, albeit sensitive. He was trying to overcome his touchiness, and immediately regretted his outburst toward the M.E.

"No, I don't know her, but there is something familiar about her. Do you think she was a rape victim?"

The coroner was making a cursory examination while he talked. "At first blush, I'd say 'No.' Her clothes are all intact, including her panties. I'll be able to say for sure after my examination."

Carlos took the usual Polaroid shots of the victim and the surrounding area, and the ambulance took the body away. He was watching the ambulance pull out onto the highway when something caught his eye. He walked a few feet down the road and plucked a flowered scarf off a creosote bush.

That afternoon the medical examiner called L.B. "The *senorita* found in the ditch this morning died from suffocation, although her neck had been broken also."

"Sounds like she was thrown from a car into the ditch."

"Yeah. That's what I think happened."

"How old do you think she was?"

"Hard to say, but the development of the body would lead me to think she was over sixteen, but under twenty. She'd been dead about five or six hours—give or take an hour or so."

"Had she been raped?"

"No, although she wasn't a virgin."

"Is there anything else I should know before I get your written report?"

"Well," the M.E. added, "this has nothing to do with her murder, but she had hepatitis A."

"That's a problem with the liver, isn't it?"

"Yes. It's mainly contracted by water or food being contaminated with human feces. I swear, the hygiene habits of some people..." The coroner's voice trailed off as he thought of the horrors afflicting people in certain parts of the world. "How are you going to find out who she was, L.B.?"

"Right now, I don't know," L.B. sighed as he spoke. "She may have been here illegally."

"That was my first guess, too."

"That's almost a certainty if no one comes forward to report a missing person."

Chapter Nine

Beauford Dornan's mother and father had died within six months of each other a little over a year ago. His three sisters and two brothers, all happily married, with children, had decided that Beau was entitled to the family homestead since he had looked after the parents during their declining years. Beau's siblings were all hoping he'd get married and settle down.

He was in the process of remodeling the old house. It had been built back in the early fifties and the wiring, plumbing, heating, cooling, and roof all needed to be upgraded. Beau was doing most of the work himself in his spare time, and many of the supplies he needed he obtained from *Juan's (You Name It, We Got It) Surplus Corner*.

On Saturday morning when Beau arrived at the secondhand store to pick up what he would need for the weekend, Juan rushed up to him waving his arms.

"Beau, look at all these people," Juan breathlessly said. "There seems to be a rush on secondhand stuff today." *Surplus Corner* was indeed crowded. "Could you help me out for a few minutes? Out on the dock?"

"Sure," Beau answered. "What d'ya want me to do?"

"There's a guy who just bought two refrigerators and two stoves. I was going to help him load them onto his pickup truck, but I can't ignore these other customers. Could you help him load them?"

"Glad to help," Beau said. "I'm not in any hurry."

Beau walked through the store and out the back door onto the loading dock. A big, brawny man was struggling with one of the stoves, trying to push it from the dock onto his truck.

"Here," Beau said. "Let me give you a hand. Hold on a minute. There's a dolly just inside."

Beau brought out the dolly and the two men had the appliances loaded within a few minutes.

"You must have a big house if you need two stoves and two fridges," Beau said.

The other man laughed. "No, I own the trailer park out on Highway 90, and most of the trailers are rentals. I always get used appliances, 'cause the renters don't take care of 'em anyway."

"How're you gonna get 'em off your truck when you get to the park?"

"I'm hopin' there'll be somebody around to help. Or, say, if you got nothin' better to do, how about followin' me and givin' me another hand? I'll be glad to pay ya for your help."

"That's not necessary, but maybe you could pop for a cuppa coffee."

"I'll do better'n that. How about a beer?"

"Just lead the way," Beau said.

After unloading the truck, the two men went into a doublewide trailer, and the owner of the park got them each a beer. Beau looked around at the furnishings and the layout of the trailer.

"Pretty nice. I'm fixin' up an old house. Maybe I'll sell it and move into one of these. By the way," Beau said, as he stuck out his hand. "Name's Beauford Dornan, but everybody calls me Beau."

The owner of the trailer park shook Beau's hand and said, "I'm Butch Flaherty, but everybody calls me Butch Cassidy. Glad to meetcha."

"How long ya been in Sierra Vista?" Beau asked.

"About ten years. Came here from St. Louis to be near my sister. I used to be a long-haul driver, but the drivin' and settin' all day finally got the best of me. I bought this court for a song, and it makes a livin'."

"Where 'bouts does your sister live?"

Butch stared out the window for a few minutes before he answered. "She's dead."

"Sorry to hear that," Beau said. "I just lost my parents about a year ago. It's tough when you're close to someone. 'Course, my folks were pretty old and they'd been sick a long time. Your sister musta been young when she died."

"She was forty-five. Her husband was the same age."

"Is he dead, too?" Beau's curiosity was getting the better of his good manners. He was thinking of his sisters and brothers and their spouses. They were all older than he, but were in the best of health.

"Yes," Butch replied. "They were both gunned down. In Naco. Five years ago."

"I remember when that happened. So the woman was your sister!"

"Yeah, and the Mexican authorities never did a damned thing about it, but if it takes the rest of my life, someone is gonna pay."

Chapter Ten

"**M**s. Roberts speaking."

L.B. smiled to himself as he heard the voice of his former secretary when she answered the phone. Sissy Roberts was an Army brat, as well as a rebel, so when her father was transferred from Fort Huachuca to Germany, she appealed to an aunt to take her in, at least until she finished high school. The aunt gladly obliged and Sissy started working in the sheriff's office after she received her diploma.

L.B. recognized her potential and urged her to take night courses in computer programming at Cochise College. After two years she had become quite a hacker, and decided she should move to Tucson where, as she told L.B. "the action is, plus the money." L.B. realized his budget wouldn't allow him to pay her what she could make in the big city, so he reluctantly gave the telephone company a glowing reference when she applied there for a job.

"Sissy," he said into the phone, "this is L.B."

"Well, Sheriff Sturling, how in the hell is my favorite ex-boss, and how is that wonderful wife of yours?"

"We're both just fine. Sissy, I need a favor."

"Oh-oh. You want me to do something illegal or immoral, I bet."

"No, nothing illegal or immoral, but perhaps unethical."

"Okay then. Fire away."

"I have two unlisted telephone numbers, and I'd like to know who they belong to."

There was a moment of hesitation, and then Sissy said, "Let me get this straight. You have two phone numbers, and you want to know who they belong to."

"That's right."

"Why don't you just punch in the numbers and see who answers?"

L.B. could almost hear Sissy adding, "You dumb shit," when he realized how ridiculous his request must sound. "Look, sissy, I know you think you're one of the original Whiz Kids, but I'm on an investigation and my calling the numbers would be counterproductive."

"You don't have to use such big words. I understand. I'm just putting you on. Give me the numbers and I'll get back with you, but you understand, Sheriff, this is going to cost you."

L.B. gave Sissy the numbers which Beau had copied from the telephone in Charlie Auchenbach's library. She promised to get back with him as soon as she had the information.

L.B. and Laurie were relaxing in their living room when the doorbell rang. He was annoyed at the interruption. He'd been reading the evening paper while listening to a classical recording. Laurie put down the mystery novel she was reading and laid her glasses on the end table. They both went to the door.

When L.B. turned on the entry light it made a halo over Sissy's head. How inappropriate, he thought, but he grinned at the pixie who was saluting him.

"Get on in here," he said.

She pounced through the door and hugged L.B. while she held out her hand to Laurie, and then hugged her and kissed her on the cheek. "You two look great," she said. "They're all wrong. I think crime does pay. Either that or you have a couple portraits stashed in your attic."

L.B. peered at Sissy over the top of his glasses. "I would have thought," he said, "rather than Oscar Wilde, your literary tastes would be more along the lines of comic books."

"Pound!" Laurie cried.

Now it was Sissy's turn to peer first at Laurie, and then at L.B. "Oh," she finally said. "Now I get it! 'L.B.' is the abbreviation for 'Pound.'" She started laughing. "And your last name is 'Sturling'! Cool! Why didn't I ever hear that before?"

"There's something I want you to be sure to remember, young lady," L.B. admonished their guest. "Only Laurie and a *very* few close friends are allowed to call me 'Pound.' So watch yourself."

Sissy saluted him again, and he led her into the living room. He turned off the stereo, and Laurie went to the kitchen to make a pot of tea.

"We're glad to see you," L.B. said, "but you didn't need to make a trip here from Tucson. You could have phoned."

"I know, but I'm spending the night with a friend here in town. We're going to catch up on all the latest gossip."

"Did you find out who those phone numbers belong to?"

"Sure," Sissy responded as she bit into a cookie and took a sip of tea.

"Well, dammit, tell me."

"Okay, okay. Keep your shirt on. Here's the scoop. The first number is listed under the name *Waterman Manufacturing Company*." She paused to consult a notebook she had taken from her handbag. "And the other is listed for *Morgenthau Enterprises*."

"I've never heard of either of them," L.B. said, and looked at Laurie who shook her head.

"Neither has our cross-reference index. There were no addresses listed, but as you know, the prefixes are Sierra Vista numbers. But," Sissy continued, "let me ask you something. What was the name of that dead dude you found at Dragoon Industries?"

"Charles Auchenbach. Why?"

"He's the cat who paid the installation costs, and the monthly bills are sent to his home address."

L.B.'s secretary informed her boss that Mr. Pizzaro was calling from St. Louis.

"I have the names of the companies Charles Auchenbach worked for before he joined Dragoon," Ramon Pizzaro said after they had dispensed with the social amenities.

"Let me guess, Sir. Were they *Waterman Manufacturing* and *Morgenthau Enterprises*, by chance?"

"Yes, that's right. May I ask how you know?"

L.B. told Mr. Pizzaro about the two extra phone lines going into Auchenbach's library at his home, and what he had found out from Sissy Roberts. "Do you have the names of the people you talked to at these alleged companies?" he asked.

"In one instance I spoke to a Mrs. Robinson, supposedly the assistant to the director of personnel at Waterman. At Morgenthau, I talked to the secretary of the manager of human resources. According to my notes, both the executives were going to be out of their offices for two weeks or so. The women gave such glowing accounts that I felt there was no need to wait until I could speak with the principals. I really feel the fool for being taken in so thoroughly."

L.B. picked up his phone and punched in a number.

"Uh...Morgenthau Enterprises," a woman said when she answered.

"This is Sheriff Sturling, Mrs. Auchenbach. How are you today?"

On the other end of the line, the receiver was slammed down. The sheriff grinned and rubbed his ear.

L.B. had hoped to find out something about Charles Auchenbach from his former places of employment, but when that turned out to be impossible, he asked Carlos for the names of some of the people who served on the Mexican-American Unity League, hoping one of them could throw some light on the murder victim. Carlos recounted the names of several Anglos in the League, and when he mentioned Pete Porter, L.B. stopped him.

Pete Porter, the attorney for the League, was a good friend of the Sturling's. Pete and his wife, Shirley, played Bridge with L.B. and Laurie once or twice a month. They rarely "talked shop," whenever they played cards, so the sheriff was unaware of Pete's civic activities.

"Sure, I knew the asshole," Pete said while he and L.B. were having coffee in a restaurant near the lawyer's office.

"Why do you call him that?" The sheriff asked.

"Because that's what he was. I imagine the only reason he belonged to the League was because of Dragoon's maquiladora."

"Was he very active in the League?"

"No. He attended as few meetings as he thought he could get by with. I know calling him an asshole isn't speaking well of the dead, but—what the hell—he can't sue me. You should have heard some of the things he said about people."

"Like what, for instance?"

"A good example is what he called that deputy of yours."

"Carlos Soto?"

"Yeah. Carlos is a good kid, and he does a super job interpreting for the League. But whenever Auchenbach thought Carlos was out of earshot, he called him a smart-assed Mexican. I was always afraid Carlos would get wind of it. I don't know how your deputy would have taken it."

"Carlos does have a pretty short fuse where his heritage is concerned. Someone else told me Auchenbach was a bigot. Do you think he was?"

"Hell, yes. He didn't seem to have any use for Mexicans or Blacks. I asked him one time why he hadn't returned the phone call I'd made to him earlier that day, and he said, 'Because that black-assed African-American in my office never gave me the message, that's why.' I knew he had an Anglo secretary, but he liked putting the blame on Lisa Webster, just so he could use that expression."

Back in his office, L.B. was musing over Pete's remarks. Auchenbach had called Carlos a smart-assed Mexican, and had referred to Lisa Webster as a black-assed African-American. And that, he thought to himself, accounts for *SAM* being written after Carlos's name, and *BAAA* appearing after Lisa's name on the list he had found in Auchenbach's desk.

Chapter Eleven

The road to Thunder Mountain Hospital wound through mesquite trees and scrub brush for about five miles off the highway. L.B. and Beau approached the two-story stucco building at ten o'clock in the morning. The tranquil surroundings and green landscaping seemed more appropriate for a classy resort than for a medical facility.

"Why would anybody build a hospital out here in the boonies?" Beau asked.

"It used to be a resort hotel, but apparently there was a water problem and they had to close," L.B. replied. "According to what I learned from the town fathers, when the hospital bought the land and the building, the water problem was cleared up."

"Convenient, I'd say."

The patients' parking lot was empty except for a late-model Cadillac with Minnesota license plates and a Lincoln Continental bearing Louisiana plates. There were no signs indicating an emergency entrance, and L.B. noticed there was no ambulance, at least that he could see.

"The people who come here must have bucks," Beau said as he parked in the lot marked for visitors.

L.B. thought he could hear sounds of laughter coming from behind the hospital as they neared the main entrance. The front door opened onto a lobby carpeted in red plush. A circular stairway leading to a mezzanine floor was covered in bright green plush. Potted palms in large terra cotta planters flanked the stairway.

"Nice colors," Beau whispered to his boss as they approached the receptionist's area, "if Christmas is your favorite holiday."

The receptionist's desk was surrounded on three sides with a four-foot high, *faux* marble partition. A woman with a forlorn look on her face, frizzled hair, and frumpy attire sighed as she stood when L.B. and Beau walked towards her. They both thought she looked a little out of place in such opulent surroundings.

"May I help you?" she sighed again, and pushed a strand of hair away from her face.

"We have an appointment to see Doctor Clevenger," L.B. replied and handed her his card.

"Oh, yes." She looked at the card and handed it back to him as though it might be contaminated. After a brief phone call she sat back down in her chair and rearranged some papers before she finally said, "Nurse Bassett will be right down."

L.B. looked for signs of blood dripping from her hands. He was sure a stigmata would be noticeable on such a penitent creature.

While they waited for Nurse Bassett, L.B. walked over to the area beneath the staircase. Floor-to-ceiling windows looked out on a large swimming pool in a courtyard behind the hospital. At the shallow end of the pool, a male nurse was bending the legs of another man who hung onto the sides of the pool. At the deep end several young people were diving, swimming, laughing, and splashing.

Nurse Bassett arrived in a few minutes. She scowled at the elderly receptionist, looked L.B. and Beau up and down, and with no acknowledgement said, "This way."

They followed her up the stairs and down a hall. She knocked on a door and entered without waiting for a response. She walked over to a chair near a window, and sat down.

The doctor stood and shook hands with L.B. and Beau and invited them to sit down. Doctor Clevenger was in his late forties or early fifties. His temples were just beginning to change from light brown to gray. L.B. judged him to be about five feet, ten inches tall. On the other hand, Nurse Bassett was close to six feet, and looked as though she pumped iron every day. She certainly wasn't struck with beauty. A formidable personage, L.B. thought to himself.

"Now, what can I do for you, Sheriff?" Doctor Clevenger asked.

"I'm sorry I had to insist on talking to you in person," L.B. replied. "We're investigating the murder of Charles Auchenbach, and we're talking to everyone he was connected with. I understand he was on your board of directors." The doctor nodded. "What can you tell me about him?"

"Not a whole lot, I'm afraid," the doctor answered. "Yes, he was a member of our board, and we're certainly going to miss him."

"How long have you known him?" L.B. was trying to read the diplomas on the wall behind the doctor's desk, but the print was too small. He silently cursed himself for leaving his glasses on the desk in his office.

"Let's see. About five years, I guess." The doctor glanced over at Nurse Bassett, and she nodded her head.

"That would be before he joined Dragoon."

"That's right. He was a consultant for one or two companies in Sierra Vista prior to going with Dragoon, if I recall."

"Would that have been with Waterman and Morgenthau?" L.B. was wondering if Auchenbach had pulled the wool over the doctor's eyes as he had Ramon Pizzaro's.

"I really don't remember," the doctor replied.

"When is the last time you saw Charles Auchenbach?"

"At our September board meeting. It was held," the doctor flipped through a calendar on his desk, "two weeks ago. The last Monday in September. Charlie was a very private person," he added. "I really know nothing about his personal life or habits."

"I'd like the names of your other board members, if you don't mind. Perhaps they might know something about him."

"There aren't all that many. Besides Charlie, there's myself, of course, Nurse Bassett," he nodded in the nurse's direction, "and Donald Norman from Bisbee."

Beau had been taking notes while the doctor and L.B. talked. The sheriff was proud of his deputy when he showed no sign of recognition at the name *Donald Norman*.

"How about you, Ms. Bassett?" L.B. said, addressing the nurse. "Can you tell me anything about Charles Auchenbach?"

"No, I know nothing about him," was her curt reply.

"How large is your hospital?" L.B. asked. "How many beds?"

The doctor smiled. "Is this part of your investigation?"

"No, of course not. I was just curious. Until a few days ago, I had no idea there was a hospital out here. Your parking lot seems rather empty. I was wondering how business is."

"We're quite small, actually. We're a twelve-bed hospital. We believe in quality, not quantity."

"If I get sick, can I come here?"

At this question, the doctor laughed. "Not unless you need to dry out, want to lose weight, or have a chronic arthritic condition. You don't look as though you're suffering from any of those maladies."

"At least not the first two, but I may not be long for the third. By the same token, though, the young people I saw in the swimming pool don't look as though they're afflicted with those infirmities."

Throughout the dialogue between the sheriff and the doctor, Beau had stolen a few glances at Nurse Bassett. Whenever he looked her way she was glaring either at him or the sheriff. On a score of one to ten, Beau thought she would probably take the prize in uglies. What is it they say, he asked himself, about people taking on the characteristics of their names? She really does look like a bassett hound.

"The youngsters you saw," Doctor Clevenger replied, "are the hired help. They do the cleaning, the laundry, the cooking—

under the supervision of a nutritionist, of course—and the gardening and anything else of the manual labor variety. It takes a lot of people to keep a facility even this small in operation."

"It didn't look as though they were doing much manual labor in the swimming pool."

The doctor glanced at his watch. At first L.B. thought this was Clevenger's way of terminating the interview. "They're on their break," the doctor explained. "We allow them the use of the facilities during their breaks and when their work is caught up. Helps morale, you know."

Beau noticed that the doctor glanced toward Nurse Bassett, and she gave him an almost indiscernible nod. She excused herself, and left the room.

"Yes, I guess it would help employee morale," L.B. agreed, "but getting back to Charles Auchenbach, are you aware of any enemies he might have had?"

"As I said, I really know nothing about him personally, Sheriff. You could have saved yourself a trip if you had let me know what your visit was about."

Nurse Bassett returned and escorted L.B. and Beau back to the reception area. As they were walking across the lobby to the door, another nurse passed them. L.B. mentally decided she wouldn't take any beauty prizes either. He noticed that Nurse Bassett lingered near the receptionist's desk until they were out the door.

As they were driving back to Sierra Vista, Beau said to L.B., "They seem to have a lot more people to do manual labor than they have nurses to look after the patients."

"As the doctor said, it takes a lot of people to maintain an establishment like that, even if they do only have twelve beds."

"I'm glad none of the patients are seriously ill. I don't see how anybody could get well if they had to look at those ugly nurses. I didn't see any other doctors," Beau continued. "D'ya suppose Clevenger is the only one on the staff?"

"I didn't want to pry too much into the workings of the hospital. I'll get hold of a physician friend of mine and see what he can tell me about that outfit."

"Did you happen to notice that all the so-called *manual laborers* looked like young Mexicans?"

"No, I really didn't notice. I was more concerned as to why the hospital had so many young patients until the doctor explained they were the hired help."

"I wonder if they could be illegals? They weren't in the pool when we left, and did you notice that that ugly nurse left the room after you asked the doc about the kids?"

"That's a good point, Beau. When we get back, get hold of Carlos and see if he knows anything about those young people working there. In the meantime, I think I'd better have a chat with Donald Norman. It's quite a coincidence that a member of the hospital's board of directors found the body of a young Mexican woman in a ditch."

"Yeah," Beau agreed. "I didn't like the way that guy acted when I first met him."

Chapter Twelve

"It's a Fat Farm," Dr. Jim Tanner responded to L.B.'s query about Thunder Mountain Hospital, confirming what Dr. Clevenger had told the sheriff.

"What do you know about Doctor Clevenger?"

"Not much, really. He doesn't come to any of our physicians' meetings. I understand he isn't married, but he doesn't seem to socialize at all."

"What about other doctors connected with the place?"

"There are a couple sort of on call, but I don't know their names or anything about them."

"Don't they play golf?"

Dr. Tanner chuckled. "No, L.B., why do you ask that?"

"I though all doctors played golf."

"If Clevenger and his cohorts do, they must have a private course. What's this all about anyway?"

"I'm not sure just yet. Do you ever refer any of your patients to Thunder Mountain Hospital?"

"I tried to once. I was treating a woman who needed some concentrated diet, nutrition, and exercise regimentation. I called

Clevenger to see if I could get her into his hospital. He apologized, but said he was all filled up for the next six months. I haven't tried to refer anyone else since then. He's probably always that busy."

"He told me the hospital has only twelve beds. If he's that busy, I wonder why he doesn't expand?"

"Probably doesn't need to. From what I hear, the place is terrible pricey. A colleague of mine tried to refer one of his patients there, and was also told there was a six-month wait. However, when the patient found out what it was going to cost, he said 'no way,' and according to my colleague, his patient is no pauper. I've been told by some other medical people that most of Thunder Mountain's patients come from outside Arizona."

L.B. remembered the out-of-state license plates he and Beau had seen on the two automobiles in the hospital's parking lot, "Maybe," he said to Tanner, "no one in Arizona can afford to go there."

L.B. had been subpoenaed to appear in court in Bisbee, the County Seat of Cochise County, and after testifying in behalf of the prosecution, he decided to make a call on Donald Norman.

The sheriff located the office of Norman and Norman, Attorneys-at-Law, on a side street in Bisbee. After identifying himself to the secretary, he was escorted into the office of Donald Norman. Norman rose and shook hands with the sheriff, and immediately started denying any knowledge of the woman's body he had seen in the ditch near Nicksville.

"I'd like some other information if you don't mind, Mr. Norman," L.B. interrupted. "We're investigating the murder of Charles Auchenbach."

"Oh...uh...I see," Norman stammered, "but what has that to do with me?"

"I thought perhaps you could tell me something about him."

L.B. thought from the look Norman gave him that the attorney thought the sheriff had just landed from outer space.

"I repeat," Norman said, "What has that to do with me? I never heard of the man until I read in the paper about his death."

"But you're on the board of directors of Thunder Mountain Hospital, aren't you?"

"Wherever did you get that idea? And what has that to do with Auchen...whatever his name is?"

"I spoke to Doctor Clevenger, the physician in charge, and he said you were one of four members on the board, along with Charles Auchenbach."

"He's mistaken. I know nothing about that hospital. I'm not even sure where it is."

"The plaque on the front of this building is inscribed 'Norman and Norman, Attorneys-at-Law.' Who is the other 'Norman'?"

"That's my father. He's retired now, but for business purposes we've retained the name 'Norman and Norman.'"

"Then perhaps it's your father who's a member of the hospital's board."

"He might be. I don't keep up with his outside activities." Norman started shuffling papers on his desk and didn't look at L.B.

"You mentioned your father is retired. Where might I find him?"

"Look, Sheriff," Norman nervously answered. "He's very ill right now. He recently suffered a heart attack, and he's in intensive care in the Copper Queen Hospital here in Bisbee."

"Hmmm," L.B. said, knowing full well that a fat farm wouldn't take a cardiac patient, "if he *is* on the board of Thunder Mountain, I wonder why he didn't go to that hospital?"

"It's too far away."

"I thought you didn't know where it is," L.B. countered.

"Uh...what I mean is, the attack was sudden, and I had to get him to the nearest facility."

***

L.B. drove to the Copper Queen Hospital, and verified that the senior Donald Norman was, indeed, in the ICU. He'd been brought in early in the morning two days ago. His condition was listed as critical.

Chapter Thirteen

Carlos drove back to Naco on the off chance of seeing Juanita again. He parked on a side street and waited until the day shift got off work. He saw the lead man, Hernando Rodriquez, get in his pickup and drive away. The deputy eased his car around the corner just as Juanita came out of the plant.

She ran over to where Carlos was parked, and without waiting for an invitation she opened the door, got into the car, sat down, and started crying.

Carlos put his arms around her while she sobbed against his shoulder. When she finally settled down, she started to apologize for her behavior.

"Just tell me what's bothering you." Carlos asked her in Spanish. "Why are you crying?"

"It's Gabriella. She called the *candida* night before last."

"You finally heard from her. That's great! What did she have to say?"

"She was very frightened when she called. She was almost hysterical," Juanita sobbed. "She said the doctor was terribly angry with her."

"Why?"

"Because she didn't pass her physical examination."

"Why would that make the doctor angry?"

"She didn't know, but she said he cursed her, he cursed Mexico, and he cursed her boyfriend."

"What about her boyfriend? Was he with her when she called?"

"No. That's another reason she's so upset. She hasn't seen him for three days. She's afraid something has happened to him."

"Do you know where she was calling from?"

"No, but she said she would meet me at the *canidida*. Then she said she couldn't talk any longer and hung up."

Juanita started crying again, and between her sobs she told Carlos that Gabriella had never shown up.

Carefully, and almost apologetically, Carlos described the skirt of the young Mexican girl who had been found in the ditch and the scarf he had found on a bush a few yards from the victim. He asked Juanita if her sister had a skirt and a scarf of that sort.

Juanita's tears stopped immediately, and she stared at Carlos. "You've seen Gabriella! Where is she?"

"Yes," was all Juanita said when she looked at the body in the mortuary. She got down on her knees and said a silent prayer for her sister. After she had made the sign of the cross, Carlos helped her to her feet. He steered her to a nearby restaurant where he ordered coffee for both of them.

"What happened to her?" she asked.

Carlos explained as delicately as he knew how, the circumstances surrounding the discovery of Gabriella's body. "Try to think of anything else she might have said," he urged Juanita, while they waited for their coffee.

"I've tried, honestly. I've racked my brain. She was so terribly frightened. Do you think she was on her way back to Naco when she was..."

"We don't know. We're trying to find out what happened. What is her boyfriend's name?"

"I don't know his last name. His first name is Raoul."

"Do you know where he's from? Where his folks live?"

"He told Gabriella his folks were dead. The only family he ever mentioned is the cousin you spoke to at the maquiladora."

The waiter brought the coffee, and Carlos waited until he had walked out of earshot. "Did she ever tell you how she planned to get across the border?"

Juanita hung her head. "I think," she said, almost whispering, "they sneaked across somewhere around Aqua Prieta."

Carlos was well aware of the illegal border crossings into Arizona made by hundreds of Mexicans each week. Since a wall had been erected in Nogalas to deter illegal crossings, the area around Naco and another Mexican border town, Aqua Prieta, were being used more and more by the Mexican Nationals who were eager to enter the United States.

"Or maybe," Juanita continued, "someone brought them over the same way you brought me across tonight."

"But you happen to be with a deputy sheriff, and the border guards know me. They also know I'll be bringing you back."

"I don't want to go back!" She was almost screaming. "I know I could pass the physical examination. I've never had hepatitis."

Carlos took Juanita's hand in his. "Juanita, you know I have to take you back, but first, tell me again what Gabriella said about not passing the physical examination."

She pulled her hand away from Carlos's. "She couldn't understand why the doctor became so angry. He had been so nice to her and her boyfriend in the beginning."

"Did she say where this examination was held?"

"No, just that it was somewhere out in the country, at a hospital. She talked about the good things she and her boyfriend had to eat.

They even got to go swimming every day while they waited for their turn."

"I don't understand," Carlos said after he had told L.B. the identity of the dead girl in the ditch, and about his conversation with Juanita. "What is all this business about taking a physical exam before you can start studying to become a United States citizen?"

"Did you read Beau's report about the young Mexicans we saw at Thunder Mountain Hospital?"

"Yes, but I haven't had a chance to get out there and talk to them. "Wait a minute," he snapped his fingers as he spoke. "Beau said there were quite a few of them in the swimming pool. Is that what you're getting at?"

L.B. nodded. "So Doctor Clevenger employs cheap labor. I can understand their having to take a physical exam, since they're working in a hospital. But it sounds as though they've been lied to about becoming citizens. I wonder what Gabriella meant when she told Juanita they could go swimming while they waited their turn. Their turn for what?"

"I'd better get out there right away." Carlos took off before L.B. had an opportunity to give him a different assignment.

What will I do with those Mexican kids, Carlos asked himself, if they are illegals? The hospital administrator has to know it's unlawful to hire undocumented immigrants. There'd be no point taking them back across the border. They'd only sneak back into the U.S. the first chance they get.

He almost missed the turnoff for Thunder Mountain Hospital during his woolgathering, and he took the corner faster than he normally would. Luckily, he didn't hit the pickup truck standing at the side of the road. The hood of the truck was up and a tall, heavyset man was tinkering with the motor. Carlos drove on. He was so intent on his mission he didn't want to stop. But, he thought, if that pickup is still there when I come back, I'll see if that guy can use some help. He glanced in his rearview mirror and saw that the man was watching him.

As Carlos walked through the front door of the hospital, a man in a white coat was coming down the stairs.

"May I help you? I'm Doctor Clevenger," the man said. He did not offer to shake hands with the deputy.

Carlos introduced himself and showed his identification to the doctor. "The sheriff's department has reason to believe that you may be employing illegal immigrants. I'd like to talk to the Mexicans who are working here."

"I'd like to talk to them, too," the doctor said. "After the sheriff and the other deputy were here the other day, they all took off."

"Then they are illegals."

"Oh, no, no." the doctor expounded. "They all had their green cards. Nevertheless, they get a little squeamish where the law is concerned."

"Was one of them named Raoul?"

"Who knows," the doctor said. "We have had Raouls, Juans, Magdalenas, Rosemarias—they come and they go. I don't have time to learn their names."

"How about a Gabriella?" Carlos asked. "Have you ever had anyone working here by that name?" Carlos watched the doctor closely, but there was not even the flicker of an eyelid.

"My concern, as I'm sure you must appreciate, is with our patients, not the hired help."

"And all of them are gone?" Carlos found this hard to believe. "Do you know where they went?"

The doctor shook his head. "Every last one of them is gone. I have no idea where they went. It's so hard to get good, dependable help these days."

Carlos left the hospital and drove back toward the highway. The pickup truck was still there; the heavyset man was still bending over the engine.

"Can I help with anything?" Carlos yelled as he rolled down the window of his car.

"No thanks. I just got it," the man answered. "There," he said, as he banged the hood down.

Carlos waited on the highway until the pickup started toward the hospital. No wonder, the deputy thought to himself, none of those kids were around. When I passed that guy on the way in, he alerted the good doctor. I wonder where the illegals could be hiding?

Chapter Fourteen

When L.B. came out of the bathroom after showering, shaving, and dressing, he was surprised to find Laurie still in bed. He knew something had to be wrong. She was rarely sick. In fact, the last time he could remember that she was still in bed after six o'clock in the morning was the day she had to have her appendix removed.

"What's the matter, Sweetie? Feeling under the weather?"

"Oh, Pound," she said with a nasal twang while she started to get out of bed, "I've caught a darn cold. My nose is stuffed up, my eyes are watering, my head hurts..."

"Stay in bed," he said, and gently pushed her back down. "I'll eat breakfast downtown. Are you sure you'll be all right? Do you want to me to get someone to come in and stay with you?"

She started to shake her head, but realized it hurt too badly. "No, I'll be okay." She pulled the sheet and thermal blanket up under her chin.

"How about if I call Mildred Johnson and ask her to come over and take care of you?"

"That's not funny, Pound. Go away. I'll be all right."

He put his hand on her forehead. "You do seem to be running a fever. I'll get some of those cold tablets for you."

He went to the kitchen and rummaged around in the drawer where they kept first-aid supplies, aspirins, and various other over-the-counter medications. He returned to the bedroom with a thermos bottle filled with orange juice and a package of cold medicine. He fluffed up her pillow, and put the one from his side of the bed under her head also.

"Here," he said, shaking two pills into the palm of her hand. He poured a glass of juice and waited while she took the medication. "Now drink some of this every time you wake up, and in four hours take two more pills. Is there anything else I can do before I leave?"

"I was going to the grocery store this afternoon. The list is over there on the chest of drawers. Could you stop on your way home and pick up those few things?"

"Sure." He found the folded sheet of paper and stuck it in his shirt pocket. He leaned down and kissed her cheek. "You just stay in bed. See you tonight." As he reached the bedroom door, he looked back. Laurie was already asleep.

L.B. looked up from the report he was reading when his secretary cleared her throat. She was standing in the doorway, and Donald Norman, the younger, was standing directly behind her.

"Mr. Norman would like to talk to you, Sheriff," his secretary said, and walked back to her desk.

L.B. nodded for Norman to take a seat. "What did you want to see me about?"

The attorney was fidgeting with his necktie and smoothing his hair. "My father died last night."

"I'm sorry to hear that." L.B. didn't know what else to say, and wondered why Norman had made the trip to Sierra Vista to let him know.

"I have some information for you, but I don't want any publicity smearing my father's name—or mine for that matter."

"If you have information which you think I should have, fine. But I cannot promise you anonymity. I think you're probably wasting your time and mine. Do I make myself clear?"

"Perfectly," Norman answered, and got up to leave. L.B. watched the lawyer go to the door, but then he turned back. "Oh, hell. I've got to get this off my chest."

"Close the door, and come back and sit down." L.B. took a tape recorder out of his desk drawer, and turned it on.

Norman cleared his throat, and started talking. "I think I may have caused my father's fatal heart attack."

"That would be pretty hard for anyone to prove," L.B. sympathized. "If you're having feelings of remorse because he died, I imagine you'll get over it after a while."

"Just hear me out, please."

L.B. nodded and sat back in his chair while Norman composed his thoughts.

"My father threw that young woman into the ditch." Norman held up his hand for L.B. not to interrupt. "He was blackmailed into doing it. He would never have done anything like that, otherwise." Norman rubbed his forehead and then rested his head in his hand before he continued. "I should explain, I guess, that my father and I live together. Mother died a few years ago—kidney failure—and I've never married. I've just kept living at home."

L.B. waited until Donald Norman finally continued talking.

"I had gotten up quite early that morning."

"The morning the young woman was found in the ditch?"

Norman nodded. L.B. pointed to the tape recorder and Norman said, "Yes. I had wakened with a headache and couldn't get back to sleep. I took a couple aspirins and was waiting for some coffee to drip when my father pulled into the driveway. I couldn't imagine where he had been at that hour. He was all disheveled and was shaking like a leaf when he walked into the kitchen.

"Did you ask him where he'd been?"

"That's the problem. I didn't ask. I *demanded* to know where he'd been. I screamed at him. I kept pressing him. He finally broke down and told me he had thrown a dead woman into the ditch near Nicksville."

"He said she was dead when he threw her into the ditch?"

"Yes. We had a hell of an argument after that. He said he'd been forced to do it, but wouldn't say who had made him do it, or why. He said everything he'd done since Mother died had been for me. I didn't know what he was talking about." Norman's voice broke before he went on. "I don't really know all I said to him, but I'm sure it was terribly unkind. While I was ranting and raving at him, he grabbed his chest. I guess the rest is history."

Norman put his head in his hands, and L.B. waited to speak until the lawyer looked up. It was almost as though he was waiting to be accused of something.

"Your seeing the body in the ditch was no happenstance, was it?"

"No. I had to see for myself what he'd done, and I felt obligated to notify your office."

L.B. reached over to turn off the tape recorder, but Norman stayed his hand. "There's more."

"Okay. Go on then."

"After he was rushed to the hospital, they told me there was nothing I could do by staying around. That's when I drove to where he said the body was, and after I notified your office I went back home. I started going through things in his study to see if I could fathom what had made him do such a thing. In his appointment book there was a notation that he was to attend a board of directors meeting at Thunder Mountain Hospital the night before." Norman stopped talking and waited as though he expected a comment from L.B.

"So?"

"His bed had never been slept in, and remember, I said he drove into the driveway a little after five in the morning."

"And you think he was at the hospital all night?"

"I think the body came from Thunder Mountain Hospital, and he was either there all night or driving around looking for somewhere to dispose of the body."

"Did he ever talk about the hospital? As a director, what was his function?"

"He never talked about it. Once, when I asked, he told me who the other board members were."

"Did he every say anything about them? About Charles Auchenbach, for instance?"

"No. I didn't lie to you the other day, Sheriff. The only thing he ever said about any of the board members was that he couldn't stand Nurse Bassett or Digger O'Dell."

"Digger O'Dell?"

"That's what my father called the mortician from Tucson."

"This mortician—he's on the board of Thunder Mountain Hospital?"

"That's what my father told me. Digger owns Memories Funeral Home and Crematorium. I think his name is really Richard Meeker."

That's interesting, L.B. thought. I wonder why Dr. Clevenger failed to mention Meeker. "Do you know how your father became involved with the hospital?"

"He got on the board after Mother's death. I thought his interest was due, perhaps, to the hospital being engaged in kidney research."

"As I understand it, the hospital is a fat farm."

"Yes, I know that's what it's supposed to be, but I now think that's just a cover."

"If it isn't a fat farm, then what do you think it is?"

"I don't know. But don't you see? That hospital is the last place my father had been."

"As far as you know."

Norman was not to be deterred. "I'm positive that someone at the hospital forced him—blackmailed him—into getting rid of that young woman's body."

Driving home that evening, L.B. kept turning over Norman's accusations in his mind when suddenly he remembered he was supposed to stop at the market for Laurie. He found a parking place and while he was walking to the door of the grocery store, he pulled Laurie's list out of his pocket.

He located a cart with four good wheels which didn't squeak too loudly and started down one of the aisles. While he was looking at Laurie's grocery list, he stopped so quickly that a woman behind him almost ran into him. She said something under her breath, pulled her cart back and went on around him. Laurie's list was nothing but a bunch of chicken scratches. Now where, L.B. wondered, have I seen something like this before?

He guessed he'd picked up the wrong sheet of paper from the top of the chest of drawers that morning. He continued on down the aisles, making his own selections. In the freezer section he found two almost palatable looking frozen dinners. I'll fix these for us tonight, he said to himself. She won't feel like cooking. And I'd better get some more frozen orange juice.

Laurie was sitting on the patio when he got home. The temperature was in the low eighties, but she was wrapped in a quilted robe and had on fur-lined slippers. Her nose was red, but her eyes had stopped watering.

L.B. kissed her on the cheek. "Your fever's down. How do you feel? Your nose is awfully red."

"I'm kinda washed out, and I think I could use a nose transplant, I've blown it so much. Did you get the things on my list?"

"Sweetie, I must have picked up the wrong sheet of paper or else you didn't make out a shopping list."

"Of course I made out a shopping list. I put it on the chest of drawers last night."

L.B. shrugged, and handed the paper to her. She unfolded it, and started laughing. "Gosh, Pound, I'm sorry. I wrote the things I needed in shorthand. I was feeling so lousy this morning I didn't remember. Now what am I going to fix for supper?"

"Don't worry about it. I picked up a couple frozen dinners. You just sit right there. They'll be ready in about forty minutes."

While L.B. was waiting for the dinners to heat in the oven, he suddenly remembered the remark Beau had made about the "chicken scratches" in Sam Babcock's diary. He rushed out to the patio. "Laurie, can one person read another person's shorthand?"

"It's possible. If they both know the same system, and if it's written accurately," she answered with a puzzled look at her husband.

"What do you mean, *the same system*?"

"Well, there's Gregg and Pitman and Speedwriting, that I know of. There may be others. But recording machines are used more widely now, and along with voice mail, E-mail, faxes, and probably a lot of things I haven't heard of, shorthand is practically a thing of the past. Why do you ask?"

"Beau said the notations in Sam Babcock's calendar looked like 'chicken scratches.' Could her notes have been written in shorthand?"

Laurie was thoughtful for about a minute. "Sam was about my age. She probably learned the Gregg system like I did. Bring her calendar home, and let's see if I can decipher it."

Laurie thought she should sleep in the guest room because of her stopped-up nose and occasional cough, but L.B. wouldn't think of it. He had trouble getting to sleep, though. His mind whipped back and forth between Charles Auchenbach, Sam Babcock, the two Donald Normans, and Thunder Mountain Hospital.

Finally, Laurie's steady breathing lulled him to sleep, but he dreamed that Carlos and Beau were running around Dragoon Industries following chicken scratches in the carpeted offices.

Chapter Fifteen

"The turnoff is right up here, isn't it?" Carlos asked. Beau nodded. "I wonder," he continued, "why there's no sign indicating that a hospital is down this road."

"Come to think of it," Beau said, "there's no sign on the building or the grounds, either." Beau turned onto the road leading to Thunder Mountain Hospital. It was a little before midnight. The two deputies had decided to see if they could locate the Mexican youngsters somewhere around the hospital. It didn't seem likely that they had left the confines of the hospital grounds. The hospital was too isolated and too far off the main road for them to hitch rides.

"What happens if we get caught?" Beau asked his partner. He was worried that their clandestine activities, being done without L.B.'s knowledge, would get them in a heap of trouble. They were both off duty, and had argued from about eight o'clock until now about this sojourn. Carlos was so insistent that Beau finally gave in, but he wasn't happy about it.

"As I told you before," Carlos answered, "the idea is to *not* get caught. There surely won't be too many people on duty this time of night. Maybe just a few nurses."

"Yeah, I guess you're right. None of those so-called patients are actually sick so they don't need round-the-clock care, but they just might try to bribe us into bringing them some cookies or candy or booze." Beau started laughing, and Carlos asked him what was so funny. "Wait 'til you see the nurses. If they're like the ones on day duty, they're really ugly."

"Let's just hope they don't see us," Carlos answered. "You'd better pull up over there in that clearing, and park behind those trees at the back." He pointed to a spot a little ways off the side of the road. It was about two city blocks from the hospital. Beau drove his Jeep around a boulder, and parked behind a stand of cottonwood trees.

Carlos had noticed a motion security light over the front entrance when he had visited the hospital yesterday. The two deputies kept well away from the front of the building, and quietly approached the back service entrance. The rear of the hospital was only dimly lit, but they hugged the walls as they made their way to the service door.

Silently, they scrambled behind a dumpster when the back door opened. An orderly walked over to the dumpster and tossed a plastic bag into it. He was the same man Beau had seen in the pool helping a patient exercise his legs.

Carlos picked up a rock and threw it. It landed about ten yards from the hospital door onto the blacktop, making just enough noise to pique the orderly's curiosity. He walked to the edge of the blacktop, and then further into the grounds surrounding the hospital.

Beau and Carlos took the opportunity to sneak into the building. The orderly had thrown a switch disconnecting the security alarm before he'd come outside. Now that they were inside, Carlos and Beau both wondered how they'd be able to leave the hospital without alerting anyone.

Carlos pointed to himself and then to a staircase leading to the basement. Beau nodded and hurried to the other end of the hall to avoid the orderly who was coming back into the building. Beau stealthily made his way up the stairs to the second floor.

Carlos crept down to the basement, and put his ear to one of the closed doors. Hearing nothing, he turned the knob. The door opened into a room filled with filing cabinets. He wasn't interested in looking at medical records, so he closed the door and went to the next one. This room was a laboratory. Vials of blood, urine, and other things the deputy didn't care to look at were in glass-doored cabinets. Petri dishes containing samples of some vile looking stuff were in glass-doored refrigerators. Microscopes and computers sat on stainless steel tables in the middle of the room.

Behind a third door was a small room with twin beds and two dressers. Door four revealed the same type of furnishings. Rooms five, six, and seven were more elaborately furnished, with carpeted floors and curtains at the windows. At the end of the basement was a large bathroom with toilets, urinals, and showers. Off to the side, a laundry room held several industrial-sized washers and dryers and cupboards containing bed linen, bath linen, and hospital gowns and robes.

Carlos sneaked back up the stairway and made his way to the darkened reception area. A sliver of light was coming from under a door off to the east side of the lobby. He could hear two people speaking, but couldn't make out what they were saying. There was enough moonlight coming through the floor-to-ceiling windows that he could just make out the word "Cafeteria" above the door. Must be some of the help having a midnight snack, he said to himself. But they weren't Mexican. They were speaking English with no accent.

Suddenly, out of nowhere, an arm encircled Carlos's neck, catching him in a vise grip while a hand covered his mouth. "Let's get the hell out of here," Beau whispered into Carlos's ear, "and I mean NOW!"

Beau released his Little Buddy, but Carlos started to walk back toward the cafeteria. He wasn't ready to leave. He had found nothing indicating there had ever been any illegal immigrants working at the hospital.

Beau waved his arms and mouthed "come on," urging Carlos to follow him. Carlos saw Beau head for the back door of the hospital, and realized he had to follow his partner whether he wanted to or not. When Beau crashed though the back door and the alarm went off in a loud screech, both deputies took off like marathon sprinters in the summer Olympics.

In the grove of cottonwoods they stopped to catch their breath, and saw the lights of an automobile careening down the road towards the highway.

"They may be looking for us, but more than likely they're on their way to alert that doctor," Beau said.

"I'd say they're probably on their way to the sheriff's office to report a break-in" Carlos responded.

"Oh, come on, Little Buddy, why would they drive to the sheriff's office. Why not phone?"

"Why not phone the doctor?" Carlos asked.

"I'll tell you why. They've got to get everybody who works there together so they can get their ducks in a row. No," Beau added, "they won't be getting' hold of the sheriff. That goddamn outfit sure as hell doesn't want any cops out here."

"Why? Did you find out something about the illegals?"

"You ain't gonna believe what I saw."

"I hope it's more than I found. Nothing. Zilch."

Before Beau got into the Jeep, he reached inside and took a pack of cigarettes from the glove compartment. He stuck one in his mouth, lit it, and put the pack in his shirt pocket.

"I thought you quit," Carlos said.

"I keep one pack around for when I'm stressed out."

Carlos had noticed Beau's hands shaking when he started to light the cigarette. "Do you want me to drive?" he asked his partner.

"No," Beau answered and walked around the Jeep and got inside, "but I just gotta sit here for a minute or two."

"Beau, what in the hell is wrong? Why were you in such a hurry to leave? You didn't give me time enough to find anything."

Beau took a long drag on his cigarette. "Carlos," he finally said as he exhaled, "I want you to promise me that you won't do anything irrational when I tell you what I saw."

"Oh, for God's sake, get on with it."

"That place ain't no fat farm."

"So what? I thought we were looking for illegal immigrants."

"Just hear me out. I sneaked up to the second floor where I figured the patients would be. After a minute or so, the nurse left her station and went down the front stairway. I guess it was time for her coffee break. I thought maybe one of the patients could tell me something about those Mexican youngsters." He rolled down the window of the Jeep and tossed his cigarette onto the gravel. "I looked in all the rooms. There were only two patients on the entire second floor. One was an older man, and the other was a woman who looked to be about fifty-five. I thought it seemed kinda strange for a fat farm, 'cause they were both hooked up to monitors and I.V.'s. They were both asleep—probably drugged, now that I think about it—so I read their charts."

"Well, Doctor Dornan, what did the charts tell you?" Carlos was immediately sorry he had made a flippant remark, because he was sure he saw tears in his partner's eyes.

"There was a lot of medical jargon on the charts, of course, and a bunch of numbers I figured had to do with vital signs." Beau stopped talking, and let out a deep sigh.

"And?" Carlos asked impatiently.

"The old man had a liver transplant day before yesterday, and the woman had a kidney transplant three days ago." Beau put his head down on the steering wheel, and wouldn't look at Carlos.

It took a few seconds for the impact of what Beau had said to sink in. "Oh my God. Are...you...absolutely...sure?" Carlos haltingly asked his partner.

Beau looked up at Carlos, put his hands on his shoulders, and nodded his head.

"How can you be so certain?" Carlos chokingly asked.

"On one chart under the word 'donor' the name 'Montoya," was written, along with 'female, blood type O.' The donor on the other one," Beau continued, never taking his eyes off Carlos, "was 'Gonzalez, male, blood type B negative.'"

Chapter Sixteen

Ramon Pizzaro looked around the apartment Arturo Garcia had rented for himself in Sierra Vista. The one-bedroom, sitting room, kitchen, breakfast nook, and bath were adequate for a bachelor, but certainly not extravagant.

Ramon smiled to himself. Although he had practically adopted Arturo when the youngster's parents had been assassinated, Arturo had never taken advantage of his benefactor. Ramon had paid the boy's college tuition and room and board, had given him spending money, which, he found out, the young man had held onto frugally, and made sure he had a job during summer vacations. Arturo's holidays from school were spent with Ramon and his daughter, Elena. Eventually Arturo and Elena fell in love. Their marriage was to take place in St. Louis in mid-November.

"I'd like to stay and visit," the older man said to Arturo, "but I have to leave for a while. I may be gone until around eight o'clock. Will you be here then?"

"Yes, I'll be here, and I'll be wide awake. I'm so excited about marrying Elena, it's hard for me to get to sleep. But, I must say, Sir, you seem terribly preoccupied. Is anything wrong? Is there anything I can do?"

"No, no, but I appreciate your concern." Ramon rubbed his forehead before he continued talking. "It's just that a very good friend of mine died a few days ago. The widow brought his ashes here from St. Louis—as her husband had requested—and she's asked me to go with her to sprinkle them around Ramsey Canyon. It turns out that's where he proposed to her. I'm not looking forward to the task."

"I can certainly understand that. What happened to your friend? How did he die?"

"He had had a heart transplant. Everything seemed to be going all right, but apparently there were complications after a time, and his body rejected the transplanted heart."

"That is sad," Arturo murmured.

When Ramon Pizzaro returned to Arturo's apartment, he looked worried and drawn. Arturo thought he had aged ten years in the short time he had been gone.

"What is it, Sir?" Arturo asked.

"Nothing I can do anything about," Ramon replied. He sat down on the couch and put his feet up on the ottoman.

Arturo fixed them each a vodka and tonic. Ramon gratefully accepted the drink. "Did you learn anything more from your friend's widow?" Arturo asked.

"Yes, and it really is disturbing me."

"Would you care to talk about it?" Ramon had always been Arturo's mentor and Father Confessor, but now the roles were reversed.

The older man settled back on the couch. "You may or may not know," he said, "there's a central clearing house in this country for organ transplants. It's known as the OTN—Organ Transplant Network. Patients in need of a transplant are put on a list—on a computer, of course. Presently that list consists of over thirty thousand names. Transplants are supposed to be on a first-come, first-serve basis, except younger people get priority. My friend's name was on that list, but he was about two thousand from the top."

"Then how did he get his transplant so soon?" Arturo asked.

"That's what is so strange. His wife—widow—didn't know he had gotten it until he returned from what she thought was a long business trip. He'd been gone about two months. He'd call her often, saying things were going well, and she thought he was talking about his business. When he got home, he told his wife he'd circumvented the system. He seemed perfectly okay, but said he just had to take it easy for a few weeks. He'd been home about a month, and one night he just died—quite suddenly." Ramon handed Arturo his glass.

"That must have been an awful shock for her," Arturo said as he handed Ramon another drink.

The older man nodded. "That wasn't the only shock. While she was at her attorney's office, trying to settle her husband's estate, they discovered that two months ago he had sold a half million dollars worth of stock. The proceeds from that sale cannot be found."

"Do you think the money was used to circumvent the OTN system?"

"It certainly looks that way."

"Since he died so suddenly, do you think the widow has grounds for a malpractice suit?"

Ramon shook his head. "He wouldn't tell her where he'd gotten the transplant."

L.B. listened to Donald Norman's tape several times. Why, he asked himself, would someone at Thunder Mountain Hospital force Donald Norman Senior into disposing of a body? It didn't make sense. And why did he toss the body into a ditch? Did he want it to be found? And soon? And did this have anything to do with Charles

Auchenbach's death? And what about Sam Babcock's murder? He couldn't believe there was a tie-in.

One thing L.B had not pursued was the statement Norman, Senior had made to his son during their heated argument: *Everything I've done since your mother's death has been for you.* L.B. picked up the phone and called Norman, Junior, asking him to come back to the sheriff's office.

"I've been thinking about that remark myself," the lawyer said, "I hate to besmirch my father's name, but. . ."

"Why don't you tell me what's on your mind." L.B. said.

"I think my father may have been involved in something illegal to make enough money to pay for my potential physical problem."

"What problem is that, if you don't mind my asking?"

"I mentioned during our other meeting that my mother died of kidney failure." L.B. nodded. Norman continued: "By the time her problem was properly diagnosed, her name was too far down the list to receive a transplant in time to save her life."

"What has that to do with your potential physical problem?"

"When I was quite young, I had to have one of my kidneys removed. An inherited problem, I guess. My father was always concerned that some day I'd need a transplant."

"And you think," L.B. interjected, "he wanted to have enough money to bribe someone to get your name to the top of the transplant list if that happened?"

Norman sadly nodded his head. "One thing I know for sure. He left me such a sizeable estate, I may have trouble paying my taxes."

"Very nice for you, I'd say," L.B. commented, wishing he had such troubles.

"Except for one thing."

"What's that?"

"I don't know where the money came from."

"And that's why you think your father was involved in something illegal?"

Norman nodded. "You see, for the last several years, on a monthly basis, thirty thousand dollars have been deposited in a Swiss bank account. Plus, sizable amounts of money—just under the ten thousand dollar limit—have been deposited in banks both here and in Tucson, and I can't find where my father got that kind of money."

"Perhaps he was a wise investor."

Donald Norman shook his head. "All his stock certificates are in his safe deposit box, and the dividends from those are accounted for."

"What about his broker? Don't they sometimes hold certificates?"

"I've checked with him. He isn't holding any."

"Did your father's tax returns reflect the money as income?"

"No. That's what I meant about not being able to pay the taxes. It's all such a mess I may have to hire an attorney." Donald Norman smiled at his own wry joke.

L.B. obtained a court order to take a look at Charles Auchenbach's bank accounts. Every month for the past five years, deposits just under ten thousand dollars had been put in one or the other of his various accounts.

Mrs. Auchenbach claimed to have no knowledge of a Swiss bank account in good old Charlie's name.

Chapter Seventeen

"Y ou did *what*?" L.B. roared at Carlos and Beau. They had just told him about their midnight trip to Thunder Mountain Hospital and what Beau had found there.

"But, Boss..." Carlos started.

"Don't—don't say anything," L.B. fumed. "I had a talk with Donald Norman yesterday, and I was trying to put something together to show 'probable cause' in order to go to Thunder Mountain Hospital with a warrant. Now you two," he paused, emphasizing his anger to glare at them, "have really bollixed things up."

"Well, gee, Sheriff..." Beau started, and then decided to drop whatever he was going to say. The look on L.B.'s face would have frozen raindrops at the Equator.

"But, Boss..." Carlos repeated, but then stopped talking.

"You saw two charts!" L.B. screamed. "You have no proof that something is amiss. And even if there is, you know damn well it would be thrown out of court because you...you..." He was so angry he couldn't finish the sentence. "If I weren't so damned short-handed, I'd suspend both of you. Get out of here. There must be someone committing a simple misdemeanor that you two can handle."

Carlos and Beau hurriedly made their exit from the sheriff's office. They got in their squad car and drove out of the parking lot. Carlos parked on a side street, and they both sat staring out the windshield. Finally, in frustration, Carlos hit the dashboard with his fist. "Dammit, what are we going to do now? How are we going to convince the boss? It all ties together, including Juanita's sister being dumped in the ditch. Since she had hepatitis, she couldn't be a donor."

"Why didn't you remind L.B. of that?" Beau asked.

"God, how could I? He was so angry I thought he was going to blow a fuse."

"Hey, Little Buddy, I think he did blow a fuse. There ain't nothin' we can do right now. Let's wait a couple days, and after he simmers down maybe we can talk to him again."

L.B., also, had been thinking about the young woman who had been found in the ditch, and about all the things Donald Norman had told him. He decided he'd see if he could get a search warrant for Thunder Mountain Hospital.

His request to the judge was met with incredulity.

"You want me to issue a search warrant based on the disappearance of a few Mexican Nationals, and the fact that a Bisbee lawyer *may* need a kidney transplant at some future date?" The judge snorted as he spoke.

"The Mexican Nationals have disappeared, and we know for a fact..."

"They could have gone anywhere! Those young folks could be in San Francisco or Denver by now. You, of all people," His Honor said as he waved his arms in the air, "know what the illegal immigration situation is. And as far as what that lawyer said about the girl in the ditch—that's hearsay."

"What about the deposits to Norman's and Auchenbach's bank accounts?"

"That's an IRS problem. You don't have probable cause, and I'm busy. Good afternoon."

When L.B. arrived home that evening, Laurie was poring over Sam Babcock's calendar. She was sitting at the kitchen table with a glass of orange juice in her hand and a box of tissues within easy reach. She grabbed a tissue and sneezed, and looked up at L.B. with watery eyes.

"How're you feeling?" he asked, as he leaned over to kiss her forehead. "You don't seem to be running a temperature."

"I'm a lot better, although I know I don't look it. But I'm having a heck of a time with Sam's shorthand."

"Why is that? I thought you said if the system was the same, you could read it. Isn't it the same system?" he grumbled.

"Pound, what's wrong? You look like a thundercloud, and sound as though you're mad at the world."

"I'm sorry, Sweetie," he said, and took her hand in his. She listened, without interrupting, while L.B. told her about his deputies' escapade at Thunder Mountain Hospital. She was appalled at the conclusions they had drawn, but being married to L.B. all these years, she knew his hands were tied for the time being.

"Enough of that," he said. "If I keep thinking about what they did, I'll get an ulcer. Now tell me why you're having trouble with Sam's diary."

"Let me give you a quick course in Steno 101," Laurie said, as she grabbed a tissue and sneezed again.

"I can hardly wait."

"Lesson number 1: the length of the strokes, the size of the circles and loops, and the angle of the lines mean different letters or words." She demonstrated some examples.

"It sounds to me almost like a foreign language. I don't see how anyone can read it."

"Lesson number 2: when you're taking dictation, you *hear* what you are writing, so you know the context when you're transcribing. The same thing holds true when you write a note to yourself. But when you try to read someone else's or when it's cold, it gets a little tricky. It's worse than reading poor penmanship when you're not familiar with it."

"I wonder if you'll find any clues to her death when you do figure it out. Oh, by the way," he added, changing the subject. "One nice thing did happen today."

"What's that?"

"Ramon Pizzaro called me just before I left the office. He wants us to be sure to attend Arturo and Elena's wedding in St. Louis in November. We'll be getting an invitation soon. I sure hope we have Auchenbach's murder cleared up before then."

"Can we afford two round-trip tickets and a hotel?" Laurie, always the practical one in the family, asked.

"No problem. He said Mark James—Dragoon's pilot—will fly us there and back in the company jet, and he wants us as guests in his home."

Laurie sat back in her chair and stared at her husband.

"What's the matter?" he asked. "Don't you want to rub elbows with the rich and famous?"

"No, no," she answered. "It's not that, but who did you say the company pilot is?"

"His name's Mark James. Why?"

Laurie grabbed Sam Babcock's calendar, and turned the pages back to three or four days before Sam was murdered. "I think," she said, "I've just figured out Sam's shorthand."

"So?" L.B. frowned at his wife as he spoke.

"Look here," she said, and then added. "Oh, never mind. You wouldn't know what to look for. Normally proper names are designated by two small diagonal lines under the word. I guess Sam didn't take the time to add them." Laurie studied the pages for a few more minutes, took off her glasses and frowned at L.B. "Do you happen to know what Mark James's wife's name is?"

"Now how would I know that? I haven't talked to him all that many times, and we've certainly never discussed his family. Although," L.B. added, remembering the time he sat with Mark in the cafeteria, "I did happen to see her picture once. She's a beautiful woman. What are you driving at?"

"Well, if her name is Marylin, then she's a patient in some hospital."

"You figured that out from those chicken scratches in Sam's calendar?"

Laurie nodded. "I'm sure this note says, 'see if Marylin James is a patient at hospital. Look up records.'"

"What day is that written on?" L.B. asked.

"It's written on the sheet for Friday, the twenty-first."

"That's strange. Sam was a volunteer at the Desert View Mental Hospital on Thursday, not Fridays, but the records at that hospital would surely be the only ones she would have access to."

"Supposing the pilot's wife is a patient there," Laurie said, "What has that to do with Sam's murder?"

"I don't know," L.B. answered, "but I guess it's worth looking into."

Laurie continued to examine the pages in the calendar. "Wait a minute, Pound," she said very quietly, "here's something else. The next day—on Saturday—there's a notation which reads, 'Mark James—seven p.m.'"

Chapter Eighteen

"Ms. Webster," L.B. said, after making yet another trip to Dragoon Industries, "there's some information I need, but you absolutely must not discuss what I ask you with anyone else. Especially anyone from Dragoon."

"If it's corporate secrets, I'm afraid I won't be much help," Lisa joked. "I don't know any."

"No, it's not that. It's about one of the employees. If necessary, I'm sure I can get an okay from Mr. Pizzaro for you to let me have access to one of the personnel files."

"He's already told all of us to cooperate with you and your deputies any way we can. Let's go into my office. The personnel files are all there." Lisa led the way to her office. One entire wall was lined with four-drawer filing cabinets. "Whose file are you interested in?"

"I'd like to take a look at Mark James's."

Lisa gave L.B. a puzzled look, and then started riffling through the file folders. She found the pilot's, laid it on her desk and opened it. "That's strange," she said. "There's no background information in here. Just the original application, performance evaluations, and a copy of the sheet we issue to get new employees onto the payroll."

"What I'm really interested in is what his wife's first name is. Is that information in there?"

"I can tell you that without looking. It's Marylin."

"Do the employees at Dragoon have medical coverage as a fringe benefit?"

"Oh, yes," Lisa answered. "We have excellent coverage. Why do you ask?"

L.B. ignored her question. "Does the medical coverage include mental health care?"

"Yes, it does. What are you getting at?"

"Sorry," L.B. answered. "I can't discuss it, and remember, neither can you. Don't even mention that I asked. Where are the records kept pertaining to insurance claims that have been submitted to your carrier?"

"They would be in this folder. But there aren't any insurance claims for Mark."

"What about Mrs. James? Any claims for her?"

Lisa went through the papers in Mark James's folder again. "No claims for Marylin, either."

"Could they be filed somewhere else? You mentioned that the background information on Mark James is missing. Could insurance claims be filed with other papers?"

"Not to my knowledge. I have no idea where the rest of his file might be. I'm quite sure, though, he hasn't submitted any insurance claims. They all have to go through me before they're sent on to the carrier. The insurance company won't deal with anyone except a designated employee. I guess it helps cut down on fraud."

"Is there any reason why Charles Auchenbach might have papers pertaining to Mark James in his office?"

"Let's take a look." L.B. and Lisa Webster went into Charlie's office and went through his desk and credenza, but no papers concerning Mark James were to be found.

"I didn't think there would be," L.B. said. "We examined this office pretty thoroughly the day he was murdered."

"Are you sure you can't tell me what this is all about?"

L.B. shook his head and thanked her for her time. She stared after him as he left her office.

Still feeling chagrined from their dressing down by the sheriff, Beau and Carlos drove out to Dragoon Industries to talk to the day shift guard. Perhaps, they thought, if they solved the Auchenbach case they could get back in L.B.'s good graces.

While they were talking to the security officer, a gorgeous woman came through the revolving doors. All three men had watched her as she walked across the parking lot. She was wearing a beige linen suit which showed her slim figure to its full advantage. Her dark hair just touched the shoulder of the jacket. Her skin was like alabaster. She had brown eyes, perfectly even, white teeth, and as Beau told Carlos later, "the purtiest smile I've ever seen."

"I'm here to see Arturo Garcia. I'd rather not give my name," she told the guard. "It's a surprise."

Beau and Carlos both straightened their shoulders and tried to look very professional.

"Now, as I was saying," Carlos began, nudging Beau out of the way and speaking in a rather loud voice, "the morning of the murder when we first arrived on the scene. . ."

"Just hold on there a minute," the guard interrupted. "I've gotta get hold of Mr. Garcia." He called Arturo to tell him he had a visitor in the front lobby.

"We're investigating some trouble," Beau said, addressing the lovely creature and temporarily taking control away from Carlos, "which happened out here last week."

"Yes, I heard about it," the young woman said, frowning momentarily and then flashing her smile at Beau. "How is the investigation going?"

Not to be outdone, Carlos answered: "It's a slow process, but I'll probably have things wrapped up in a couple days."

Beau looked incredulously at Carlos. "I didn't know that," he exclaimed.

Carlos gave him a withering look. "You're not up to speed on all the latest developments."

"I guess not," Beau said, scratching his head, momentarily losing his official-looking demeanor.

The young woman turned from the two deputies and looked toward the elevator as the door opened.

Arturo gasped, and in three strides took her in his arms, putting his face in her hair. "Elena, Darling, it's been so long!"

"Dad told me he'd asked you to take over Mr. Auchenbach's position, and I couldn't wait to get here," she said when Arturo finally released her.

"Oh," he said, finally remembering his manners, "Beau, Carlos, may I present Elena Pizzaro, my fiancé."

She flashed her lovely smile again and said, "We've sort of met. Informally, that is."

Before Beau or Carlos could say anything, Arturo addressed his bride-to-be. "Let's go to my office. We've got wedding plans to make."

The lovers walked arm-in-arm towards the elevator. The two deputies and the guard were left standing, looking at the elevator door and at each other.

"Come on, Romeo, or should I say Sherlock," Beau said to Carlos. "Let's go back to the office, and you can fill me in on how you're gonna wrap this all up in a coupla days."

Carlos dropped Beau off at the sheriff's office, and then drove to Naco. He was curious about Hernando Rodriquez. Why had the lead man told the employees at the maquiladora that they would be blamed for what had happened to Charles Auchenbach? Why was he trying to intimidate them?

A border guard on the Mexican side of Naco was a friend of Carlos's, and he knew practically everyone in town, as well. The deputy learned from his friend that Rodriquez lived about three miles outside the small border town.

Hernando's *ranchero* consisted of several hundred acres bordered with white plank fencing. Horses, corrals, and bunkhouses could be seen in the distance. The main house looked to be about 3,000 square feet. Two small boys were running around on a green lawn yelling and laughing as they tried to avoid the sprinklers.

What sort of salary, Carlos wondered, does Dragoon pay this guy, for him to have such a lush oasis in the middle of the Sonoran Desert?

The next afternoon, Carlos drove back to Naco to keep an appointment he had made with Arturo Garcia. They met outside the maquiladora, and Carlos asked Arturo if there was a private office where they could talk.

"I'll run the lead man out onto the floor," Arturo said. "That's where he should be anyway, and we'll use his office."

After they usurped the lead man's office, Carlos told Arturo what Beau had found at the Thunder Mountain Hospital, and his suspicions that Hernando might be mixed up in all of it somehow.

Arturo was nonplussed. "Oh, my God," he exclaimed. "You are serious, aren't you?"

Carlos nodded and went on to explain the mysterious death of Gabriella, Juanita's sister, and the fact that the young woman had had hepatitis.

"So," Arturo said, "she couldn't become a donor, and she had to be disposed of. How horrible!"

"This is all supposition, so far, but there are too many coincidences, and that bothers me."

"Now let me tell you an interesting story." Arturo repeated what Ramon Pizzaro had told him about his friend's failed heart transplant and the sale of his stock which could not be accounted for. "And," Arturo added, "If illegal immigrants are being used as organ donors, it could be they are being lured to the hospital from here. That could account for our extremely high rate of attrition."

"Right," Carlos agreed. "I hadn't thought about that."

"Then what are we waiting for? Get hold of the sheriff and let's go out to that hospital." Arturo stood and started for the door.

"Sit back down and let me fill you in on how law enforcement works." He went on to tell Arturo how he and Beau were in the doghouse with their boss, and why they couldn't storm the Thunder Mountain Hospital.

They talked for another half hour or so, shook hands and left the building. Neither of them noticed Hernando Rodriquez strolling past his office door as they parted.

Chapter Nineteen

Beau got down off the ladder, and answered his phone on the third ring. "Yo," he said as he picked up the receiver.

"Hi, Beau," Butch Cassidy answered. "How'd you like to go out to the Oasis Bar for a coupla beers?"

"Why not," Beau replied. "I'm tryin' to fix some broken plaster, but I ain't gonna get done tonight anyway. But, hey, can you pick me up? My Jeep's on the blink and won't be fixed 'til tomorrow."

"Sure thing. Be at your place in about twenty minutes."

On their way to the Oasis Bar, chatting about nothing in particular, Beau suddenly said, "Hey, see that maroon Toyota that just went around us? Foller it for a while, will ya?"

Butch stayed far enough back to not be noticeably visible, but kept the Toyota in sight. "How long do you want me to tail 'im? The turnoff to the Oasis is just up the road, you know." They could see the green neon palm trees and brown neon camel in the distance on the roof of the bar. "Who's in that Toyota, anyway?"

"Just keep follerin' him. It's the guy from Dragoon that old man Pizzaro brought in."

Butch looked over at Beau, and almost ran off the road. "You're talkin' 'bout my nephew."

"Oh, shit, that's right. Where could he be goin' this time of night, and out here in the boondocks? I hope it ain't where I think it is."

"I think what he does is his own business. I feel funny doin' this. Why do you want to follow him?"

"Just keep goin'. I'll tell you later."

Before long the Toyota turned off the main highway onto the road leading to Thunder Mountain Hospital. As Butch turned onto the side road also, Beau asked him to extinguish his headlights.

"Look," Beau said, "he's stopping. We'd better, too." Soon they heard a car door slam. A coyote howling in the distance was the only other sound penetrating the stillness.

"What's that kid up to anyway?" Butch asked no one in particular. "Sounds like he got out of the car. Now what do we do?"

"I don't know what to do," Beau lamented. "I had a gut feeling he was gonna come out here. And he may be getting' into something over his head. There's some mighty strange things goin' on at that hospital."

"Beau, we've only been friends for a few weeks, and I thought you were an okay guy, but right now I feel like knockin' you on your ass if you don't come clean with me and tell me what you're talkin' about. What hospital? Are you sure there's a hospital out here? I didn't see any sign."

"I can't go into it right now. Just trust me." They both got out of Butch's pickup and walked up the road to where the empty Toyota was parked. "Damn it," Beau grumbled, "I wish I had my radio. I got the feelin' we're gonna need some back-up."

"Why would you need back-up to go to a hospital? Come to think of it, why would Arturo be way out here going to a hospital?"

"It's too long a story right now. I'll have to tell you later."

"If Arturo is in some kind of trouble..." Butch started, but Beau interrupted him.

"Look. You drive back to town. Phone the sheriff and tell im' I asked you to call. Tell him what we've seen and that things don't look right. He'll probably give you hell, but tell him I'm..."

"Gotcha," Butch interjected. "What are you gonna do in the meantime."

"I'll cut across the field to the hospital. I don't suppose you've got a gun with ya?" Beau asked.

"There's a Colt .45 in the glove compartment, and a rifle in the rack across the back window."

"I'll take the revolver," Beau said as they ran back to the truck.

When Butch handed his pistol to Beau, he said, "Just make sure you don't shoot my nephew."

Beau was across the ditch and running toward the hospital before Butch got his truck turned around to head back to Sierra Vista. Beau ignored the door leading to the reception area of the hospital and ran around the building to the back entrance where he and Carlos had gained access before.

He remembered the security alarm. Dammit, he said to himself, how am I gonna get in? Then he noticed the wires hanging loose over the door. Could Arturo have cut them? A sign on the door—which he had missed the first time he and Carlos were there—read "Authorized Personnel Only."

Well, hell, he thought, a deputy sheriff otta be "authorized." He tried the door and breathed a sigh of relief when it opened and no alarm went off. He thought he heard a thump coming from the basement, but when the noise wasn't repeated, he ignored it.

The first floor was in darkness with the exception of moonlight streaming through the floor-to-ceiling windows. He stealthily made his way up the carpeted stairway to the second floor. The door to the doctor's office was slightly ajar, and he could hear voices.

L.B. silently growled when the phone on his bedside table started to ring. "Sheriff Sturling," he grumbled. "What is it?"

"Sheriff, you don't know me, but my name is Butch Cassidy. I'm a friend of your deputy, Beau Dornan."

"Has something happened to Beau?" L.B. anxiously asked, as he sat up and started dressing as they talked.

"No, but..." Butch explained to L.B. what he knew, and told the sheriff that Beau had asked him to call.

"I'm on my way," L.B. said. "I'll have every available unit with me, but promise me something. If you see Beau before I get there, try to keep him alive. I want to kill him myself."

"Why were you trespassing on private property this time of night, Mr. Garcia?" Dr. Clevenger asked as he settled back into his swivel chair behind his desk.

Nurse Bassett had grabbed Arturo when he came through the service door, dragged him up the stairs, emptied his pockets, and bound him to a chair facing the doctor's desk. Nurse Bassett stood by the doctor's chair, her presence looming over that side of the room.

"Getting additional information on the monstrous, vile operation you're running here," Arturo replied.

"Is that so? And what might that be?" The doctor asked.

"Using illegal immigrants as organ donors."

"Oh, come on. What proof do you have?"

"Granted, it's all circumstantial right now. . ."

"Then don't you think you're being a little brash sneaking in here after hours? After all, you aren't a law enforcement officer. According to the business cards in your wallet, you're an executive at Dragoon Industries."

Arturo wondered where in the hell Carlos was. When they had met at the maquiladora in Naco, they had agreed to meet outside the hospital, to gain access somehow, and confirm what Beau had told Carlos. However, when he'd arrived there was no sign of the deputy, and that hideous nurse, who was six inches taller than Arturo and 70 pounds heavier, seemed to be waiting for him. She'd grabbed him and dragged him up to the doctor's office before he knew what was happening.

"That's right, but I think you're using Dragoon's maquiladora as a pipeline to lure illegal immigrants into this country. I always thought," Arturo continued, trying to keep the conversation going in hopes that Carlos would show up, "that a doctor's oath was to save lives."

"Supposing what you say about my using illegal aliens as donors is true," the doctor replied, "then shouldn't I be commended for saving lives? Organ transplants save many lives."

"In this instance, at the expense of other healthy human beings," Arturo spat.

"Oh, don't be so naïve. Don't you think it's more worthwhile to save the life of a scientist, a politician, a professor, to name a few, than someone coming into this country illegally?"

"Why is a scientist, a politician, or a professor more important than any other human being?"

"Because the professional people I'm talking about have something to offer society, rather than being a burden on society. You can't expect the professional people I'm speaking of to wait around for the right donor to come along. Nor should they have to wait until their names reach the top of the list."

Arturo heard Nurse Bassett suck in her breath. The doctor was admitting that Arturo's suspicions were correct, but the doctor's conceit and the ideals he thought were good for society were too great for him to remain silent.

"You've surely read about the people in India selling one of their own kidneys, so what's the big deal?"

"But that is their decision," Arturo said. "They certainly can't sell their hearts or their livers."

"It might come to that, if they need money for their families. My hospital offers transplants on demand. Therefore, there's hope for anyone who can afford it."

"You offer the illegals hope, too."

"I not only offer them hope, but a lot more. For a few weeks they live in Utopia. They have plenty to eat, clean beds to sleep in, they're able to swim in the pool, and they're given a complete physical examination to assure they are healthy."

"What if they aren't healthy? Suppose you find out one of them has a liver disease, or a heart ailment after you've lured him or her to this so-called Utopia?"

The doctor shrugged. "They, like the healthy ones, are expendable. It's as simple as that."

"How many organs does each donor supply?"

"Oh, it's a one-on-one situation. It would be entirely too exhaustive for me to attempt more than one transplant operation a day."

God, Arturo thought, I wish I were wired. But what difference does it make now? They'll probably use one of my organs, too. Where in the hell is Carlos? I've got to keep the doctor talking; stall for time.

"Are all of your operations successful?" Arturo asked, thinking of Ramon Pizzaro's friend.

"Some are, some aren't. My success ratio is better than most, however. And, of course, we have a never-ending supply of donors. And patients, I might add."

"Business doesn't seem to be too good at the moment."

"We had to suspend activities for a few days. That nosey deputy sheriff was becoming a nuisance, but as it turns out, he'll make quite a good donor himself. He looks as though he's in good physical condition, and since he's Mexican, I doubt if anyone will miss him."

Oh, God, Arturo thought to himself, Carlos was caught as well. I wonder where they've put him?

"A few years ago," Arturo said, still hoping for a miracle to get him out of this mess, "my father discovered what was going on, and you assassinated him and my mother."

"Ah, so that was your father. I'm not certain he knew exactly, but he was getting too close for comfort. But no, I didn't kill your parents. That individual who was murdered at Dragoon a couple weeks ago saw to it that someone eliminated them. We've already established that money talks, you know."

"That individual who was murdered supplied you with the illegals, didn't he?"

"Actually, the maquiladora supplies them. When the Mexican Nationals first start working at the twin plant it seems like such a great place. But soon they become disenchanted. They're made to work harder, quality control becomes more stringent, and they, of course, become greedy. A word dropped here and there by the right person, and they're ready for bigger and better dreams."

"Dreams of coming to the United States."

"What else?"

"And Charlie Auchenbach told them he'd help them when they came to the U.S..."

"Of course," the doctor chuckled as he spoke. "Charlie had his own ideas about ethnic cleansing."

"How did they get across the border? Sneak in?"

The doctor laughed. "You can't keep illegals out of this country no matter how many border guards you hire. And those fences are a joke. These people are determined to come here, and I will certainly help them get here any way I can."

"Did you kill—or did you have someone kill—Charlie Auchenbach?"

"No, no," the doctor said. "You don't kill the goose that lays the golden egg. I have no idea who would want good, old Charlie dead."

"But with him out of the picture, your supply of donors may come to a halt."

"Ha," Doctor Clevenger jeered, but with no mirth in his laugh, "Charlie couldn't carry out such an endeavor by himself. That lead man...what's his name? Oh, yes, Hernando Rodriquez. Now there's a person who is extremely loyal to his Mexican brothers and sisters. He sets up the potential candidates. Auchenbach's participation was to get the illegals from the border to the hospital. We won't have too much difficulty replacing him. Everyone is out for a quick buck, Mr. Garcia, even if it means betraying your countrymen as Rodriquez does."

"Or betraying your professional ethics," Arturo added.

The doctor suddenly turned to look at Nurse Bassett. "We've talked enough. Let's get this over with." He nodded his head toward the end of his desk where a hypodermic needle was laying.

Nurse Bassett picked up the needle, pulled at the syringe, and started around the desk toward Arturo.

Will Elena, Arturo thought to himself, ever understand why I've disappeared? God, I love her so...

Beau, who had heard most of the dialogue between the doctor and Arturo, decided now was the time to make his move. He held Butch's pistol in both hands and was just getting ready to kick the door open the rest of the way when he heard the safety being released on the gun which was touching the side of his head.

"I wouldn't do anything rash," the orderly said. "Let's you and me join the others."

The orderly took Butch's pistol out of Beau's hand and pushed him through the door. Beau stood by the chair where Arturo was bound, and the orderly walked over behind the desk.

"Well, well," Dr. Clevenger said, "what have we here?"

"What we have here," said a voice from the doorway, "is a sawed-off shotgun. Don't anybody move."

Jeee-sus, Beau thought to himself. Butch never told me about that gun and it's illegal as hell, but who gives a shit.

The doctor, the orderly, and Nurse Bassett looked locked in place, but the frozen tableau lasted only a few seconds. Nurse Bassett's hand, holding the syringe, stealthily crept toward Arturo.

"I wouldn't do that if I were you," Butch said. "This gun'll blow all of you on that side of the room off the face of the earth. Now put the syringe down, and untie Mr. Garcia. NOW!"

"Are you okay, Arturo?" L.B. asked. By the time he and his other deputies had caught up with Butch and Beau, the drama had wound down in Doctor Clevenger's office.

"Yes, I'm fine. I thought it was all over when that orderly and Beau came through the door," Arturo answered as he rubbed his wrists and ankles. "But," he said as he looked at Butch, "I don't understand what you're doing here, Uncle Oscar."

"Uncle *Oscar*?" Beau asked as he looked at his friend.

"It's 'Butch' to you, Beau," Uncle Oscar growled, and looking back at his nephew, he said, "I was just out for an evening drive and wondered what all the activity was out here at the hospital."

"Here, Uncle Os. . .Butch," Beau said, handing Butch his pistol. "Thanks for the use of your shooter."

Doctor Clevenger, Nurse Bassett, and the orderly were taken to the Cochise County Jail. L.B. wanted to question them before he turned them over to the F.B.I.

A doctor and two nurses were summoned from the city hospital in Sierra Vista to look after the two transplant patients until their conditions were stable enough for them to be moved.

* * *

"It was a very dangerous thing," L.B. admonished Arturo, "coming out here by yourself."

"Sheriff, I don't quite know how to tell you this, but I was supposed to meet Carlos here. He didn't show up, and that doctor and nurse caught me as soon as I was at the service entrance. I think Carlos may have gotten here before I did and was caught, too. The doctor said something about using him as a donor."

"Be right back," Beau shouted and started for the stairway. He hurried down to the basement where he'd heard the thump when he'd come into the hospital. He now heard sounds of kicking coming from what appeared to be a janitor's closet. The door was locked.

"Get back! I'm gonna break 'er down," Beau yelled at the closed door. His shoulder splintered the hollow-core door.

Carlos, too, had been bound to a chair, and he was gagged as well. He'd managed to tip over the chair he was tied to and had maneuvered to the door, kicking it whenever he heard movement outside.

"How'd you get yourself in this mess, Little Buddy?" Beau asked as he removed the gag.

Carlos grinned at his partner. "I wanted to wrap *something* up in a couple of days, but I didn't count on that nurse being so big and strong. And for once, you're right. She'd certainly never take any beauty prizes."

Chapter Twenty

Nurse Bassett was the personification of abject despair until L.B. told her she could hope for a lighter sentence for herself if she offered to tell all she knew. She looked at Beau for confirmation, and when he nodded she suddenly took on an attitude of coyness as though his nod had been a flirtatious action.

I guess, Beau thought to himself, this is what they mean when they say "it ain't over 'til the ugly lady sings."

Nurse Bassett batted her eyelashes at the deputy, practically ignoring L.B., and began her story:

Charles Auchenbach and Dr. Clevenger went back a long way. She didn't know whether they had been involved in other shady deals, but the good doctor and Hernando Rodriquez had set up the pipeline for Auchenbach to shuttle the illegal immigrants to Thunder Mountain Hospital even before Charlie had been hired at Dragoon Industries.

Hernando would instill in the minds of the young Mexicans working at the maquiladora the advantages of coming to the United States, becoming U.S. citizens and getting good jobs, making more money than they had ever dreamed of. He made the adventure sound like Utopia, and indeed for a while, it was.

If the immigrants were healthy they would continue to work, and play, at the hospital until the time came when one of their vital organs was needed. The work they did was not strenuous—just laborious enough to keep them occupied and to diminish their curiosity. They had absolutely no contact with the transplant patients.

The doctor normally did about two transplants a week. He didn't want so much traffic going into or out of the hospital, so he kept his operations, more or less, at a minimum. Of course, the young people made friends with their fellow countrymen, and occasionally one of the youngsters would start asking questions about why Jose, Magdalena, Maria, or Juan weren't around any longer. The curious ones were the ones who went missing next.

Unfortunately the physical exams sometimes disclosed that the immigrants had tuberculosis, hepatitis, as in the case of Gabriella, or other communicable diseases. Those youngsters had to be disposed of.

Also, if after six months or so, there wasn't a match, even the healthy ones had to be gotten rid of. It was too dangerous to keep them around for too long a time.

"How were they disposed of?" L.B. asked.

Nurse Bassett continued: many of the bodies were buried in an area east of the hospital, in a deserted part of the desert. Memories Mortuary in Tucson conveniently cremated some of the donors whenever a legitimate cremation was taking place.

Listening to Nurse Bassett's story, Beau was glad Carlos was on another assignment. L.B. had anticipated the nurse's gruesome tale, and had sent his Hispanic deputy off to the western part of the county. When the nurse mentioned the cremations, Beau thought grimly to himself: yeah, two for the price of one.

"Did Doctor Clevenger have anything to do with Donald Norman throwing Gabriella into the ditch?" If the donors' bodies were disposed of in such a cavalier fashion, L.B. couldn't see the reason for Norman's action.

Nurse Bassett nodded, smiled at Beau, and went on with her story: Gabriella became completely distraught after Dr. Clevenger berated her, her boyfriend, and Mexico in general. They were going to dispose of her the following day, but she had accidentally stumbled into the boardroom that evening. Each of the directors—Clevenger, Bassett, Norman, Meeker, and Auchenbach—thought she might have been listening at the door. In their excitement at possibly having their secret discovered, they forgot that Gabriella could neither speak nor understand English.

Clevenger had grabbed her and held onto her while Auchenbach held a sofa cushion over her nose and mouth until she suffocated.

Dr. Clevenger wanted a lawyer on the board in the event the hospital was ever taken to court. Norman had a good track record in malpractice cases, and the doctor knew the lawyer's son might someday need a kidney transplant. But the doctor couldn't stand Norman, Senior. He always was concerned that Norman might blow the whistle on the hospital's activities, and he needed another "hold" over the lawyer.

Clevenger had Nurse Bassett put Gabriella's body in the trunk of Norman's car. He told Norman to get rid of the body or he would see to it that his son never had a kidney transplant in any hospital, anywhere, in the event he ever needed it.

"What sort of money did Doctor Clevenger charge his patients for an organ transplant?" L.B. asked.

Nurse Bassett's voice droned on: the transplants ran in the neighborhood of half a million dollars. *Nice neighborhood*, Beau thought. Each director received around $50,000 a month, and Hernando Rodriquez received $10,000 for every donor he supplied.

Beau thought to himself: yeah, Mexican labor always is cheaper.

L.B. turned Dr. Clevenger and Nurse Bassett over to the F.B.I., and that agency rounded up all the other members of the Thunder Mountain Hospital staff, including the guilt-ridden receptionist who, it turned out, was the doctor's mother.

Memories Funeral Home and Donald Meeker were shut down, pending further investigation.

At last count, the remains of one hundred, forty-nine people had been dug up in an area about half a mile from the hospital. Most of the graves contained one body, but in a few instances, two, three, and four people had been buried together. The bulldozing continued.

L.B. knew that somewhere in Mexico many mothers were wondering where their teenagers were. Why hadn't they written, and why hadn't they sent for their families as they had promised?

There was no way to trace the identities of the bodies which had been uncovered, and who could say where the ashes were of those who had been cremated? The Mexican government felt the situation was not their problem, and they made little fuss.

Doesn't anyone care? I care, L.B. said to himself as he rubbed his forehead, but what can I do? Oh, God, what can any of us do?

Very shortly he thought, the media will get wind of the story and all hell will break loose. He'd see to it that his two deputies, along with Arturo and Butch Flaherty, would get credit for uncovering the scam, but he'd let the F.B.I. and I.N.S. do the talking to the press.

Chapter Twenty-one

L.B. made another trip to the mental hospital where Sam Babcock had been a volunteer. He presented a court order to the administrator who answered the sheriff's questions, albeit unwillingly.

A nurse took the sheriff down a hall to a room with one-way glass. Mark James's wife was sitting on a stool, rocking back and forth. Her arms were crossed over her chest, and she seemed to be singing to herself.

There was little resemblance to the lovely woman in the photograph which L.B. had seen in the cafeteria the day he talked to the pilot. Marylin's eyes were sunken, and the dark circles beneath them precluded the notion that they had once been a dazzling green. Her fair skin was ashen, and her gorgeous red hair had been shorn from her head.

L.B. looked questioningly at the nurse who hung her head.

"We had to shave her head. She kept pulling out her hair. It was either that or put her in a straitjacket. That seemed too cruel. She's been through enough."

***

L.B. and Ramon Pizzaro waited in the airport lobby for Mark James. The pilot was checking out one of Dragoon's jets in preparation for a flight.

The sheriff had spent about an hour filling in Ramon on what he had learned at Desert View Sanitorium and what he had pieced together concerning the murders of Charles Auchenbach and Sam Babcock.

"From what you've told me, Sheriff, I'm compelled to do everything in my power for that young man's defense."

"I understand," L.B. replied.

When Mark walked into the airport he was, as usual, dressed casually in slacks, knit shirt, and leather flight jacket. He stopped short when he saw the owner of Dragoon Industries and the sheriff waiting for him at the door.

"We need to talk to you for a few minutes, Mr. James."

L.B. motioned the two men toward a lounge off the lobby. "Why don't we go in here." He closed the door. No one said anything until the three men sat down.

"How long has your wife been in the sanitorium, Mark?" L.B. asked.

"I don't see that my wife's illness is any of your damned business," the pilot replied.

"Mark, please," Mr. Pizzaro said. "I'm distressed that you didn't confide in me as to your wife's illness. And I understand you haven't even filed a claim with our insurance company."

"It isn't something I want broadcast around."

"But her hospitalization must be terribly expensive, and our insurance company would stand most of the charges."

"I'm taking care of the expenses," Mark said. "But how did you find out my wife is...ill?" He looked at Pizzaro and then at L.B.

Mr. Pizzaro sighed and settled back in his chair. That kind and gentle man was passing the ball to the sheriff.

"Mark, isn't it true that your wife had an extremely unpleasant experience which left her mentally damaged, and," L.B.'s voice became very quiet, "you set about to get your revenge?"

Mark stood up and started pacing back and forth at the end of the room. Finally, when L.B. and Ramon said nothing, he sat down and put his head in his hands. "What the hell," he said. "She doesn't even know me any more. She's living in a never-never land, and the doctors tell me she'll never improve. Yes," he vehemently added. His hands gripped the arms of his chair and his knuckles turned white. "I got my revenge, and if I had it to do over, I'd do it again. I'm just sorry that son-of-a-bitch didn't suffer the way Marylin has, or the way I have.

"Why don't you tell us what happened?"

Mark let out a long sigh, and started his story:

"It was right after Auchenbach and I started with the company. Let's see, about six or eight months ago, I guess." He stopped talking and shook his head as he looked at both men. "It seems like an eternity. We were flying back here from St. Louis after the quarterly meeting."

"The one where I met your wife," Mr. Pizzaro added.

Mark nodded.

Pizzaro turned to L.B. and said, "Once each year when we have our quarterly meeting in March, we invite the wives. Makes it more of a social occasion."

Mark continued: "Auchenbach's wife didn't go to the meeting. All the other guys and their wives were going to stay in St. Louis and not come back for a couple days, but Auchenbach said he had an important appointment back here and had to return. Marylin wanted to come home, too. We hadn't been in our house very long, and she was still in the process of making drapes and..." Mark's voice choked, and L.B. and Ramon patiently waited until he regained his composure.

"They were the only ones on the plane—besides me, of course. We'd been up about half and hour when he started making passes at

Marylin. She didn't know what to do, but kept trying to put him off. He'd had a few drinks, and pretty soon..." Again Mark hesitated, and L.B. and Pizzaro waited. ". . . the bastard ordered her—ORDERED HER—mind you, to take off her clothes. He told her if she screamed, I'd have to leave the controls and we'd crash. She knows nothing about airplanes. She didn't know there's such a thing as automatic pilot. She believed him."

"And he raped her," L.B. added.

"He raped her, he sodomized her, he forced her to perform oral sex...you name it." Mark's voice was so low, the other two men had to strain to hear him.

"Was Marylin rational enough afterwards to tell you what had happened?" L.B. asked.

"I thought she looked a little disheveled when we got off the plane, but I figured she'd probably fallen asleep, and hadn't had time to fix her hair or makeup before we landed. Auchenbach took off in his car like a bat out of hell, and she started crying. She finally became composed enough to tell me what happened."

"In heaven's name," Mr. Pizzaro exclaimed, "why didn't you come to me and tell me?"

"I thought about it, but I wanted to confront Auchenbach first. He denied it, of course. He said Marylin's story was a frustrated woman's fantasy. I wanted to kill him then, and would have if I'd known Marylin was going to be affected to such an extent. He told me that if I did anything or said anything, he'd see to it that I never flew another airplane as long as I lived."

Mark paused before he continued: "You see, before I got this job with Dragoon I'd been with Sunbelt Airlines. Going into Salt Lake City one time, a malfunction caused me to crash. No one was killed, but a lot of people were injured—none seriously—but, of course, the lawsuits converged on Sunbelt. The crash was investigated by the FAA and God knows who all. The powers-that-be attributed it to pilot error. Now you know and I know if that were true, my license would have been pulled, or at least I'd have been suspended. Neither happened. They didn't suggest that I go through a recertification test, either. They just fired me. I didn't get the chance to explain that their damned plane needed an overhaul."

"It was after that," L.B. interjected, "that you applied at Dragoon."

"Yes, and when Auchenbach interviewed me, he knew all about the Sunbelt fiasco. He had a whole dossier on me. He said he thought I'd been railroaded. Looking back, I'm sure he wanted me to be beholden to him. For what, I have no idea. He didn't know Marylin then, so I can only guess it was some rotten scheme he was involved in."

Pizzaro and L.B. looked at each other. Both men were thinking the same thing: had it been Auchenbach's intention to have Mark James fly the Mexican Nationals into Arizona for Dr. Clevenger's use? Perhaps so, but then Charlie's lust apparently had gotten the better of him.

"You see, Sheriff," Mark's voice broke into their thoughts. "Flying is my life. Flying and Marylin."

"When did she start...er, become ill?"

"She was acting strangely almost as soon as it happened, but in a couple weeks things got really bad. I'd come home from a trip and she'd be in the nude, apparently waiting for me. But if I tried to touch her she'd scream and run and hide in the closet. I'd just have to leave her alone until she decided to come out.

"Then one day I came back from a trip, and one of our neighbors told me she'd seen Marylin out in the yard dancing and singing...with no clothes on. A couple nights later I wakened and found her gone. I really panicked, because her car was gone, too. Just then, I heard the garage door open. She parked the car and walked into the house as though nothing was out of the ordinary. The only thing is, she was stark naked.

"The next day I took her to the sanitorium to see if I could get some help for her. She has posttraumatic stress disorder, and in her case the doctors say it's hopeless." Mark looked at both men. "I guess my case is too."

L.B. decided it was time to change the conversation. "How did you get Auchenbach to go to the office so early that day?"

"I called him from St. Louis. I'd flown part of the staff there a couple days before. I gave him just an inkling of a scheme I'd heard about, and how we could make a killing. No pun intended.

"He was such an arrogant, greedy bastard, I think he'd forgotten all about what he'd done to Marylin. I told him this was something we couldn't discuss during business hours and that we'd have to meet in his office at five-thirty the next morning because I'd have to get back to St. Louis to bring everybody home.

"I got there a little before five-thirty. I rang the bell at the dock door several times to confuse Joe, the guard. Poor old Joe! He thought he was hearing bells ringing in his head. He's getting up there in years, you know, and he's scared of being let go. I figured he'd not report the ringing bells. About the third or fourth time he checked the dock, the door didn't close all the way. I shinnied under it and made my way upstairs."

"Was Auchenbach waiting for you when you got to his office?" L.B. asked.

"Yeah, and can you believe it? He was reading a girlie magazine, and asked me to look at one of the pictures. That made it easy for me. I walked behind his desk to look at the picture and...you know the rest."

"We didn't find a magazine when we examined his office," L.B. said.

"I took it with me. I thought someone might think Auchenbach was killed because he was a lech, and possibly make the connection to Marylin."

"Why did you kill Sam Babcock?"

"On Thursday I'd gone to see Marylin. Just as I was walking into the hospital, Sam was leaving. We were both pretty startled when we saw each other. I made some inquiries and found out she was a volunteer at the hospital. I was sure she'd put two and two together. I was right. She had."

"According to her calendar, you were supposed to see her on Saturday night. How did you get into Yucca Estates on Friday?"

"It was like this," Mark began. "When I had to take Marylin to the hospital, I was beside myself. Everywhere I looked something reminded me of her, and I couldn't help but think of the horror she'd gone through. I sure as hell couldn't stand the sympathetic stares of the neighbors. I hardly knew them, but still...

"I decided to look for a furnished apartment. A soldier I know from the Fort was going TDY, and he lives in Yucca Estates. He rented his unit to me. I had the phone from our house put on call forwarding to the condominium, and I had my mail forwarded to a post office box.

"Sam called me and asked if I'd like to come over and talk on Saturday. I told her 'sure,' and that I'd be there about seven. I went to her place right after she called. She didn't realize I was living over on the other street. I forced her into her den, and you know the rest of that scenario, too."

"What sort of weapon did you use?" L.B. asked.

"A stiletto. I'd picked it up in Nam and brought it home as a souvenir. I sure didn't mind using it on Auchenbach, but I wish to Christ I'd never run into Sam Babcock that day at the hospital. I threw the damned thing away. From the plane. It's lying somewhere on a prairie in Missouri."

"Mark," L.B. said, "you realize I'm going to have to take you in."

"Yeah, I know. But I really have to pee. Is it all right if I go to the restroom first?"

"Of course. We'll wait here for you."

"And," Mr. Pizzaro said, "we'll talk about getting you the best defense lawyer we can find."

"Hi, Pound," Laurie called out from the patio when L.B. walked into the house. "Come and look out back. There must be another forest fire to the north. Do you see all that smoke?"

L.B. gazed out at the mountains. He put his arm around Laurie's waist. "By the way," he said, "we won't be going to St. Louis next month after all."

"Oh, my gosh!" Laurie exclaimed. "The wedding hasn't been called off, has it?"

"No, no. It's just been postponed."

"Pound," Laurie said, examining L.B.'s face. "What happened to make those kids change their plans?"

"About an hour ago," L.B. answered, "Mark James flew the Dragoon jet into the side of the Huachuca Mountains."

~THE END~

Afterword

I wish to express my thanks to Leyla Cattan, a former columnist for the *Arizona Daily Star*, Tucson, Arizona. One of her columns was the inspiration for *The Maquiladora Murders*, and she granted permission for me to include it, in translation, herewith:

"Separating Rumor From Fact"

"In the world of information, one of the most serious responsibilities facing a journalist is being able to separate rumor from fact.

"For the last three years, and with certain frequency, I see respectable media in Latin America reporting about loathsome acts committed by U.S. authorities against children, women, and undocumented persons.

"On March 4 the daily *Excelsior of Mexico* published a story that reported serious human-rights violations against undocumented aliens along the border.

"The story included allegations of human-organ trafficking. I classify this more as rumor than fact.

"Yet my curiosity is piqued, since this isn't the first time I have heard of such things.

"The story in *Excelsior* says that the violations were revealed at the annual meeting of the Border Commission on Human Rights. The commission works closely with the Houston-based Immigration Law Enforcement Monitoring Project, which documents civil- and human-rights violations by immigration officials.

"Its coordinator, Maria Jimenez, reported that she has heard of organ trafficking, yet doesn't have any proof of its existence. She added that from May 1988 to May 1989, INS personnel allegedly committed 380 cases of rights violations—29 cases in Tucson.

"Judith Galarza, member of the Chihuahua Independent Committee for Defense of Human Rights in Ciudad Juarez, told the commission of the alleged human-organ traffic. Galarza, whose sister disappeared in 1978 in Mexico City, said that more than 1,000 people have disappeared after crossing into the United States illegally.

"She was my last hope for establishing whether human-organ traffic was rumor or fact. She still cannot document the information, so the matter is still cloudy."

About the Author

Sydnie Goodell retired from a Fortune 500 company after 31 years of service in the human resources, marketing, and administration arenas. Leaving the private sector, she pursued her hobby of writing and has been published in magazines and periodicals.

She is currently working on her second novel, "The Monsoon Murders," which is a prequel to "The Maquiladora Murders." Both books are set in Cochise County, Arizona, where the author lives with her husband.